DEATH UNDER WATER

Neither Tarzan nor the Ashairian acolytes were used to fighting under these unlikely conditions— far beneath the surface of the sacred lake, where the water slowed motion to a nightmare deliberateness, and a single rip in the protective suits would bring instant drowning.

Backed by Helen and Herkuf, he met the first assault with knife and trident—and soon five Ashairians were floating limply, their blood a spreading cloud in the murky water. Tarzan pursued the remaining enemy, who turned at bay and prepared to fight, his desperation making him the most dangerous antagonist of all.

Tarzan's fingers touched the Ashairian's wrist —he had almost succeeded in seizing the hand that held the dagger—when a giant fish struck his legs a heavy blow and upset him. As the ape-man fell backward, the Ashairian saw his opportunity. He lunged forward upon the falling Tarzan, his knife ready to plunge into his foe's heart.

Edgar Rice Burroughs

TARZAN NOVELS

now available from Ballantine Books:

COMPLETE AND UNABRIDGED!

TARZAN
and the
Forbidden City

Edgar Rice Burroughs

BALLANTINE BOOKS • NEW YORK

ISBN 0-345-25960-2

This edition published by arrangement with
Edgar Rice Burroughs, Inc.

Manufactured in the United States of America

First U.S. Printing: March 1964
Fifth U.S. Printing: August 1978

First Canadian Printing: August 1974

Cover illustration by Boris Vallejo

1

THE RAINY SEASON was over; and forest and jungle were a riot of lush green starred with myriad tropical blooms, alive with the gorgeous coloring and raucous voices of countless birds, scolding, loving, hunting, escaping; alive with chattering monkeys and buzzing insects which all seemed to be busily engaged in doing things in circles and getting nowhere, much after the fashion of their unhappy cousins who dwell in unlovely jungles of brick and marble and cement.

As much a part of the primitive scene as the trees themselves was the Lord of the Jungle, lolling at his ease on the back of Tantor, the elephant, lazing in the mottled sunlight of the noonday jungle. Apparently oblivious to all his surroundings was the ape-man, yet his every sense was alert to all that passed about him; and his hearing and his sense of smell reached out far beyond the visible scene. It was to the latter that Usha, the wind, bore a warning, to his sensitive nostrils—the scent spoor of an approaching Gomangani. Instantly Tarzan was galvanized into alert watchfulness. He did not seek to conceal himself nor escape, for he knew that only one native was approaching. Had there been more, he would have taken to the trees and watched their approach from the concealment of the foliage of some mighty patriarch of the forest, for it is only by eternal vigilance that a denizen of the jungle survives the constant threat of the greatest of all killers—man.

Tarzan seldom thought of himself as a man. From infancy he had been raised by beasts among beasts, and he had been almost full grown before he had seen a man.

Subconsciously, he classed them with Numa, the lion, and Sheeta, the panther; with Bolgani, the gorilla, and Histah, the snake, and such other blood enemies as his environment afforded.

Crouching upon the great back of Tantor, ready for any eventuality, Tarzan watched the trail along which the man was approaching. Already Tantor was becoming restless, for he, too, had caught the scent spoor of the man; but Tarzan quieted him with a word; and the huge bull, obedient, stood motionless. Presently the man appeared at a turn in the trail, and Tarzan relaxed. The native discovered the ape-man almost simultaneously, and stopped; then he ran forward and dropped to his knees in front of the Lord of the Jungle.

"Greetings, Big Bwana!" he cried.

"Greetings, Ogabi!" replied the ape-man. "Why is Ogabi here? Why is he not in his own country tending his cattle?"

"Ogabi looks for the Big Bwana." answered the black.

"Why?" demanded Tarzan.

"Ogabi has joined white bwana's safari. Ogabi, askari. White bwana Gregory send Ogabi find Tarzan."

"I don't know any white bwana, Gregory," objected the ape-man. "Why did he send you to find me?"

"White bwana send Ogabi bring Tarzan. Must see Tarzan."

"Where?" asked Tarzan.

"Big village, Loango," explained Ogabi.

Tarzan shook his head. "No," he said; "Tarzan no go."

"Bwana Gregory say Tarzan must," insisted Ogabi. "Some bwana lost; Tarzan find."

"No," repeated the ape-man. "Tarzan does not like big village. It is full of bad smells and sickness and men and other evils. Tarzan no go."

"Bwana d'Arnot say Tarzan come," added Ogabi, as though by second thought.

"D'Arnot in Loango?" demanded the ape-man. "Why didn't you say so in the first place? For bwana d'Arnot, Tarzan come."

And so, with a parting word to Tantor, Tarzan swung off along the trail in the direction of Loango, while Ogabi trotted peacefully at his heels.

*   *   *

It was hot in Loango; but that was nothing unusual, as it is always hot in Loango. However, heat in the tropics has its recompenses, one of which is a tall glass filled with shaved ice, rum, sugar, and lime juice. A group on the terrace of a small colonial hotel in Loango was enjoying several recompenses.

Captain Paul d'Arnot of the French navy stretched his long legs comfortably beneath the table and permitted his eyes to enjoy the profile of Helen Gregory as he slowly sipped his drink. Helen's profile was well worth anyone's scrutiny, and not her profile alone. Blonde, nineteen, vivacious, with a carriage and a figure charming in chic sport clothes, she was as cool and inviting as the frosted glass before her.

"Do you think this Tarzan you have sent for can find Brian, Captain d'Arnot?" she asked, turning her face toward him after a brief reverie.

"Your full face is even more beautiful than your profile," thought d'Arnot, "but I like your profile better because I can stare at it without being noticed." Aloud, he said, "There is none knows Africa better than Tarzan, Ma'moiselle; but you must remember that your brother has been missing two years. Perhaps——"

"Yes, Captain," interrupted the third member of the party, "I realize that my son may be dead; but we shan't give up hope until we *know*."

"Brian is *not* dead, Papa," insisted Helen. "I *know* it. Everyone else was accounted for. Four of the expedition were killed—the rest got out. Brian simply disappeared—vanished. The others brought back stories—weird, almost unbelievable stories. Anything might have happened to Brian, but *he is not dead!*"

"This delay is most disheartening," said Gregory. "Ogabi has been gone a week, and no Tarzan yet. He may never find him. I really think I should plan on getting started immediately. I have a good man in Wolff. He knows his Africa like a book."

"Perhaps you are right," agreed d'Arnot. "I do not wish to influence you in any way against your better judgment. If it were possible to find Tarzan, and he would accompany you, you would be much better off; but of course there is no assurance that Tarzan would agree to go with you even were Ogabi to find him."

"Oh, I think there would be no doubt on that score," replied Gregory; "I should pay him handsomely."

D'Arnot lifted a deprecating palm. *"Non! Non! mon ami!"* he exclaimed. "Never, never think of offering money to Tarzan. He would give you one look from those gray eyes of his—a look that would make you feel like an insect—and then he would fade away into the jungle, and you would never see him again. He is not as other men, Monsieur Gregory."

"Well, what can I offer him? Why should he go otherwise than for recompense?"

"For me, perhaps," said d'Arnot; "for a whim—who knows? If he chanced to take a liking for you; if he sensed adventure—oh, there are many reasons why Tarzan might take you through his forests and his jungles; but none of them is money."

At another table, at the far end of the terrace, a dark girl leaned toward her companion, a tall, thin East Indian with a short, black chin beard. "In some way one of us must get acquainted with the Gregorys, Lal Taask," she said. "Atan Thome expects us to do something besides sit on the terrace and consume Planter's Punches."

"It should be easy, Magra, for you to strike up an acquaintance with the girl," suggested Lal Taask. Suddenly his eyes went wide as he looked out across the compound toward the entrance to the hotel grounds. "Siva!" he exclaimed. "See who comes!"

The girl gasped in astonishment. "It cannot be!" she exclaimed. "And yet it is. What luck! What wonderful luck!" Her eyes shone with something more than the light of excitement.

The Gregory party, immersed in conversation, were oblivious to the approach of Tarzan and Ogabi until the latter stood beside their table. Then d'Arnot looked up and leaped to his feet. "Greetings, *mon ami!*" he cried.

As Helen Gregory looked up into the ape-man's face, her eyes went wide in astonishment and incredulity. Gregory looked stunned.

"You sent for me, Paul?" asked Tarzan.

"Yes, but first let me introduce—why, Miss Gregory! What is wrong?"

"It is Brian," said the girl in a tense whisper, "and yet it is not Brian."

"No," d'Arnot assured her, "it is not your brother. This is Tarzan of the Apes."

"A most remarkable resemblance," said Gregory, as he rose and offered his hand to the ape-man.

"Lal Taask," said Magra, "it *is* he. That is Brian Gregory."

"You are right," agreed Lal Taask. "After all these months that we have been planning, he walks right into our arms. We must get him to Atan Thome at once—but how?"

"Leave it to me," said the girl. "I have a plan. Fortunately, he has not seen us yet. He would never come if he had, for he has no reason to trust us. Come! We'll go inside; then call a boy, and I'll send him a note."

As Tarzan, d'Arnot, and the Gregorys conversed, a boy approached and handed a note to the ape-man. The latter glanced through it. "There must be some mistake," he said; "this must be meant for someone else."

"No, bwana," said the boy. "She say give it big bwana in loin cloth. No other bwana in loin cloth."

"Says she wants to see me in little salon next to the entrance," said Tarzan to d'Arnot. "Says it's very urgent. It's signed, 'An old friend'; but of course it must be a mistake. I'll go and explain."

"Be careful, Tarzan," laughed d'Arnot; "you're used only to the wilds of Africa, not to the wiles of women."

"Which are supposed to be far more dangerous," said Helen, smiling.

A slow smile lighted the face of the Lord of the Jungle as he looked down into the beautiful eyes of the girl. "That is easy to believe," he said. "I think I should warn d'Arnot."

"Oh, what Frenchman needs schooling in the ways of women?" demanded Helen. "It is the women who should be protected."

"He is very nice," she said to d'Arnot, after Tarzan had left; "but I think that one might be always a little

9

afraid of him. There is something quite grim about him, even when he smiles."

"Which is not often," said d'Arnot, "and I have never heard him laugh. But no one who is honorable need ever be afraid of Tarzan."

As Tarzan entered the small salon he saw a tall, svelte brunette standing by a table at one side of the room. What he did not see was the eye of Lal Taask at the crack of a door in the opposite wall.

"A boy brought me this note," said Tarzan. "There is some mistake. I don't know you, and you don't know me."

"There is no mistake, Brian Gregory," said Magra. "You cannot fool such an old friend as I."

Unsmiling, the ape-man's steady gaze took the girl in from head to foot; then he turned to leave the room. Another might have paused to discuss the matter, for Magra was beautiful; but not Tarzan—he had said all that there was to say, as far as he was concerned.

"Wait, Brian Gregory!" snapped Magra. "You are too impetuous. You are not going now."

Tarzan turned back, sensing a threat in her tone. "And why not?" he asked.

"Because it would be dangerous. Lal Taask is directly behind you. His pistol is almost touching your back. You are coming upstairs with me like an old friend, arm in arm; and Lal Taask will be at your back. A false move, and—poof! you are dead."

Tarzan shrugged. "Why not?" he thought. In some way these two were concerning themselves with the affairs of the Gregorys, and the Gregorys were d'Arnot's friends. Immediately the ape-man's sympathies were enlisted upon the side of the Gregorys. He took Magra's arm. "Where are we going?" he asked.

"To see another old friend, Brian Gregory," smiled Magra.

They had to cross the terrace to reach the stairway leading to the second floor of another wing of the hotel, Magra smiling and chatting gaily, Lal Taask walking close behind; but now his pistol was in his pocket.

D'Arnot looked up at them in surprise as they passed. "Ah, so it *was* an old friend," remarked Helen.

10

D'Arnot shook his head. "I do not like the looks of it," he said.

"You *have* changed, Brian Gregory," said Magra, smiling up at him, as they ascended the stairway. "And I think I like you better."

"What is this all about?" demanded Tarzan.

"Your memory shall soon be refreshed, my friend," replied the girl. "Down this hall is a door, behind the door is a man."

At the door they halted, and Magra knocked.

"Who is it?" inquired a voice from the interior of the room.

"It is I, Magra, with Lal Taask and a friend," replied the girl.

The voice bade them enter, and as the door swung open, Tarzan saw a plump, greasy, suave appearing Eurasian sitting at a table at one side of an ordinary hotel room. The man's eyes were mere slits, his lips thin. Tarzan's eyes took in the entire room with a single glance. There was a window at the opposite end; at the left, across the room from the man, was a dresser; beside it a closed door, which probably opened into an adjoining room to form a suite.

"I have found him at last, Atan Thome," said Magra.

"Ah, Brian Gregory!" exclaimed Thome. "I am glad to see you again—shall I say 'my friend'?"

"I am not Brian Gregory," said Tarzan, "and of course you know it. Tell me what you want."

"You are Brian Gregory, and I can understand that you would wish to deny it to me," sneered Thome; "and, being Brian Gregory, you know what I want. I want directions to the city of Ashair—the Forbidden City. You wrote those directions down; you made a map; I saw you. It is worth ten thousand pounds to me—that is my offer."

"I have no map. I never heard of Ashair," replied Tarzan.

Atan Thome's face registered an almost maniacal rage as he spoke rapidly to Lal Taask in a tongue that neither Tarzan nor Magra understood. The East Indian, standing behind Tarzan, whipped a long knife from beneath his coat.

"Not that, Atan Thome!" cried Magra.

11

"Why not?" demanded the man. "The gun would make too much noise. Lal Taask's knife will do the work quietly. If Gregory will not help us, he must not live to hinder us. Strike, Lal Taask!"

2

"I CANNOT UNDERSTAND," said d'Arnot, "why Tarzan went with those two. It is not like him. If ever a man were wary of strangers, it is he."

"Perhaps they were not strangers," suggested Helen. "He seemed on the best of terms with the woman. Didn't you notice how gay and friendly she appeared?"

"Yes," replied d'Arnot, "I did; but I also noticed Tarzan. Something strange is going on. I do not like it."

Even as d'Arnot was speaking, Tarzan, swift as Ara, the lightning, wheeled upon Lal Taask before the knife hand struck; and, seizing the man, lifted him above his head, while Atan Thome and Magra shrank back against the wall in stark amazement. They gasped in horror, as Tarzan hurled Lal Taask heavily to the floor.

Tarzan fixed his level gaze upon Atan Thome. "You are next," he said.

"Wait, Brian Gregory," begged Thome, backing away from the ape-man and dragging Magra with him. "Let us reason."

"I do not reason with murderers," replied Tarzan. "I kill."

"I only wish to frighten you, not to kill you," explained Atan Thome, as he continued to edge his way along the wall around the room, holding tightly to Magra's hand.

"Why?" demanded Tarzan.

"Because you have something I want—a route map to Ashair," replied Thome.

"I have no map," said Tarzan, "and once again I tell

12

you that I never heard of Ashair. What is at Ashair that you want?"

"Why quibble, Brian Gregory?" snapped Atan Thome. "You know as well as I do that what we both want in Ashair is The Father of Diamonds. Will you work with me, or shall you continue to lie?"

Tarzan shrugged. "I don't know what you're talking about," he said.

"All right, you fool," growled Thome. "If you won't work with me, you'll not live to work against me." He whipped a pistol from a shoulder holster and levelled it at the ape-man. "Take this!"

"You shan't!" cried Magra, striking the weapon up as Thome pressed the trigger; "you shall not kill Brian Gregory!"

Tarzan could not conceive what impelled this strange woman to intercede in his behalf, nor could Atan Thome, as he cursed her bitterly and dragged her through the doorway into the adjoining room before Tarzan could prevent him.

At the sound of the shot, d'Arnot, on the terrace below, leaped to his feet. "I knew it," he cried. "I knew there was something wrong."

Gregory and Helen rose to follow him. "Stay here, Helen," Gregory commanded; "we don't know what's going on up there."

"Don't be silly, Dad," replied the girl; "I'm coming with you."

Long experience had taught Gregory that the easiest way to control his daughter was to let her have her own way, inasmuch as she would have it anyway.

D'Arnot was in the upper hall calling Tarzan's name aloud by the time the Gregorys caught up with him. "I can't tell which room," he said.

"We'll have to try them all," suggested Helen.

Again d'Arnot called out to Tarzan, and this time the ape-man replied. A moment later the three stepped into the room from which his voice had come to see him trying to open a door in the left hand wall.

"What happened?" demanded d'Arnot, excitedly.

"A fellow tried to shoot me," explained Tarzan. "The

woman who sent me the note struck up his gun; then he dragged her into that room and locked the door."

"What are you going to do?" asked Gregory.

"I am going to break down the door and go in after him," replied the ape-man.

"Isn't that rather dangerous?" asked Gregory. "You say the fellow is armed."

For answer Tarzan hurled his weight against the door and sent it crashing into the next room. The ape-man leaped across the threshold. The room was vacant. "They've gone," he said.

"Stairs lead from that verandah to the service court in the rear of the hotel," said d'Arnot. "If we hurry, we might overtake them."

"No," said Tarzan; "let them go. We have Lal Taask. We can learn about the others from him." They turned back to re-enter the room they had just quitted. "We'll question him, and he'll answer." There was a grimness about his tone that, for some reason, made Helen think of a lion.

"If you didn't kill him," qualified d'Arnot.

"Evidently I didn't," replied the ape-man; "he's gone!"

"How terribly mysterious!" exclaimed Helen Gregory.

The four returned to their table on the terrace, all but Tarzan a little nervous and excited. Helen Gregory was thrilled. Here were mystery and adventure. She had hoped to find them in Africa, but not quite so far from the interior. Romance was there, too, at her elbow, sipping a cool drink; but she did not know it. Over the rim of his glass d'Arnot inspected her profile for the thousandth time.

"What did the woman look like?" Helen asked Tarzan.

"Taller than you, very black hair, slender, quite handsome," replied the ape-man.

Helen nodded. "She was sitting at that table at the end of the terrace before you came," she said. "A very foreign looking man was with her."

"That must have been Lal Taask," said Tarzan.

"She was a very striking looking girl," continued Helen. "Why in the world do you suppose she lured you to that room and then ended up by saving your life?"

Tarzan shrugged. "I know why she lured me to the

14

room, but I don't understand why she struck up Atan Thome's hand to save me."

"What did they want of you?" asked d'Arnot.

"They think I am Brian Gregory, and they want a map of the route to Ashair—The Forbidden City. According to them The Father of Diamonds is there. They say your brother made such a map. Do you know anything about it? Is this safari of yours just for the purpose of finding The Father of Diamonds?" His last query was addressed to Gregory.

"I know nothing about any Father of Diamonds," replied Gregory. "My only interest is in finding my son."

"And you have no map?"

"Yes," said Helen, "we have a very rough map that Brian drew and enclosed in the last letter we received from him. He never suspected that we'd have any use for it, and it was more by way of giving us an idea of where he was than anything else. It may not even be accurate, and it is certainly most sketchy. I kept it, however; and I still have it in my room."

"When the boy brought you the note," said d'Arnot, "you had just asked me why I had sent for you."

"Yes," said Tarzan.

"I was here in Loango on a special mission and met Monsieur and Ma'moiselle Gregory," explained d'Arnot. "I became very much interested in their problem; and when they asked me if I knew of any one who might help them find Ashair, I thought immediately of you. I do not mean that I should venture to ask you to accompany them, but I know of no one in Africa better fitted to recommend a suitable man to take charge of their safari."

That half smile that d'Arnot knew so well, and which was more of the eyes than of the lips, lighted Tarzan's face momentarily. "I understand, Paul," he said. "I will take charge of their safari."

"But that is such an imposition," exclaimed Helen. "We could never ask you to do that."

"I think it will be interesting," said Tarzan—"since I have met Magra and Lal Taask and Atan Thome. I should like to meet them again. I think if I remain with you our paths shall cross."

"I have no doubt of it," said Gregory.

"Have you made any preparations?" asked Tarzan.

"Our safari is being gathered in Bonga," replied Gregory; "and I had tentatively employed a white hunter named Wolff to take charge of it, but of course now——"

"If he will come along as a hunter, we can use him," said Tarzan.

"He is coming to the hotel in the morning. We can talk with him then. I know nothing about him, other than that he had some rather good references."

* * *

Behind Wong Feng's shop is a heavily curtained room. A red lacquer Buddha rests in a little shrine. There are some excellent bronzes, a couple of priceless screens, a few good vases; the rest is a hodge podge of papier-mâché, cheap cloisonné, and soapstone. The furniture is of teak, falling apart after the manner of Chinese furniture. Heavy hangings cover the only window, and the air is thick with incense—sticky, cloying. Atan Thome is there and Magra. The man is coldly, quietly furious.

"Why did you do it?" he demanded. "Why did you strike up my gun?"

"Because," commenced Magra; then she stopped.

" 'Because!' 'Because!' " he mimicked. "The eternal feminine. But you know what I do to traitors!" He wheeled on her suddenly. "Do you love Gregory?"

"Perhaps," she replied, "but that is my own affair. What concerns us now is getting to Ashair and getting The Father of Diamonds. The Gregorys are going there. That means they haven't the diamond, and that they do have a map. You know that Brian made a map. You saw him. We must get it, and I have a plan. Listen!" She came and leaned close to Thome and whispered rapidly.

The man listened intently, his face lighting with approval. "Splendid, my dear," he exclaimed. "Lal Taask shall do it tomorrow, if he has recovered sufficiently. Wong Feng's working on him now. But if that fails, we still have Wolff."

"If he lands the job," said Magra. "Let's have a look at Lal Taask."

They stepped into a small bedroom adjoining the room

16

in which they had been talking. A Chinese was brewing something in a kettle over an oil lamp. Lal Taask lay on a narrow cot. He looked up as the two entered.

"How are you feeling?" asked Atan Thome.

"Better, Master," replied the man.

"Him all light mollow," assured Wong Feng.

"How in the world did you escape?" asked Magra.

"I just pretended to be unconscious," replied Lal Taask, "and when they went into the next room, I crawled into a closet and hid. After dark I managed to get down into the back court and come here. I thought I was going to die though. I can almost believe that man when he says he's not Brian Gregory, unless he's developed an awful lot of strength since we saw him last."

"He's Brian Gregory all right," said Thome.

Wong poured a cupful of the concoction he had brewed and handed it to Lal Taask. "Dlink!" he said.

Lal Taask took a sip, made a wry face, and spat it out. "I can't drink that nasty stuff," he said. "What's in it?—dead cats?"

"Only li'l bit dead cat," said Wong. "You dlink!"

"No," said Lal Taask; "I'd just as soon die."

"Drink it," said Atan Thome.

Like a whipped cur, Lal Taask raised the cup to his lips and, gagging and choking, drained it.

3

THE GREGORYS, with Tarzan and d'Arnot, were breakfasting on the terrace the next morning, when Wolff arrived. Gregory introduced him to Tarzan. "One o' them wildmen," observed Wolff, noting Tarzan's loin cloth and primitive weapons. "I seen another one once, but *he* ran around on all fours and barked like a dog. You taking it with us, Mr. Gregory?"

"Tarzan will be in full charge of the safari," said Gregory.

"What?" exclaimed Wolff. "That's my job."

"It was," said Tarzan. "If you want to come along as a hunter, there's a job open for you."

Wolff thought for a moment. "I'll come," he said. "Mr. Gregory's goin' to need me plenty."

"We're leaving for Bonga on the boat tomorrow," said Tarzan. "Be there. Until then we shan't need you."

Wolff walked off grumbling to himself.

"I'm afraid you've made an enemy of him," said Gregory.

Tarzan shrugged. "I did nothing to him," he said, "but give him a job. He'll bear watching, though."

"I do not care for that fellow's looks," said d'Arnot.

"He has good recommendations," insisted Gregory.

"But he is, obviously, no gentleman," said Helen.

Her father laughed good naturedly. "But we are hiring a hunter," he said. "Whom did you expect me to sign on, the Duke of Windsor?"

"I could have stood it," laughed Helen.

"Wolff has only to obey orders and shoot straight," said Tarzan.

"He's coming back," announced d'Arnot, and the others looked up to see Wolff approaching.

"I got to thinking," he said to Gregory, "that I ought to know just where we're goin'; so I could help lay out the route. You see, we gotta be careful we don't get out o' good game country. You got a map?"

"Yes," replied Gregory. "Helen, you had it. Where is it?"

"In the top drawer of my dresser."

"Come on up, Wolff; and we'll have a look at it," said Gregory.

Gregory went directly to his daughter's room; and Wolff accompanied him, while the others remained on the terrace, chatting. The older man searched through the upper drawer of Helen's dresser for a moment, running through several papers, from among which he finally selected one.

"Here it is," he said, and spread it on a table before Wolff.

The hunter studied it for several minutes; then he shook his head. "I know the country part way," he said, "but I ain't never heard of none of these places up here —Tuen-Baka, Ashair." He pointed them out with a stubby forefinger. "Lemme take the map," he said, "and study it. I'll bring it back tomorrow."

Gregory shook his head. "You'll have plenty of time to study it with Tarzan and the rest of us on the boat to Bonga," he said; "and it's too precious—it means too much to me—to let out of my hands. Something might happen to it." He walked back to the dresser and replaced the map in the upper drawer.

"O.K.," said Wolff. "It don't make no difference, I guess. I just wanted to help all I could."

"Thanks," said Gregory; "I appreciate it."

"Well then," said Wolff, "I'll be running along. See you at the boat tomorrow."

Captain Paul d'Arnot, being of an inventive turn of mind, discovered various reasons why he should remain in the vicinity of Helen Gregory the remainder of the morning. Luncheon was easy—he simply invited the Gregorys and Tarzan to be his guests; but when the meal was over, he lost her.

"If we're leaving for Bonga tomorrow," she said, "I'm going to do some shopping right now."

"Not alone?" asked d'Arnot.

"Alone," she replied, smiling.

"Do you think it quite safe? a white woman alone," he asked. "I'll be more than glad to go with you."

Helen laughed. "No man around while I'm shopping—unless he wants to pay the bills. Goodby!"

Loango's bazaar lay along a narrow, winding street, crowded with Negroes, Chinese, East Indians, and thick with dust. It was an unsavory place of many odors—all strange to occidental nostrils and generally unpleasant. There were many jutting corners and dark doorways; and as Helen indulged the feminine predilection for shopping for something to shop for, Lal Taask, slithering from corner to doorway, followed relentlessly upon her trail.

As she neared the shop of Wong Feng, she stopped before another stall to examine some trinkets that had attracted her eye; and while she was thus engaged, Lal

Taask slipped past behind her and entered the shop of Wong Feng.

Helen dawdled a few moments before the stall; and then, unconscious of impending danger, approached the shop of Wong Feng; while, from the interior, Lal Taask watched her as a cat might watch a mouse. The girl was entirely off her guard, her mind occupied with thoughts of her shopping and anticipation of the adventurous expedition in search of her missing brother; so that she was stunned into momentary inaction and helplessness as Lal Taask seized her as she was passing the shop of Wong Feng and dragged her through the doorway into the dark interior—but only for a moment. When she realized her danger, she struggled and struck at her assailant. She tried to scream for help; but the man clapped a palm roughly over her mouth, stifling her cries, even though they would have brought no help in this vicious neighborhood.

Lal Taask was a wiry, powerful man; and Helen soon realized the futility of struggling against him as he dragged her toward the rear of the shop.

"Come quietly," he said, "and you will not be harmed."

"What do you want of me?" she asked, as he removed his palm from across her mouth.

"There is one here who would question you," replied Lal Taask. "It is not for me to explain—the master will do that. Whatever he advises will be for your own good—obey him in all things."

At the far end of the shop Lal Taask opened a door and ushered Helen into the dimly lighted room that we have seen before. Magra was standing at one side; and Helen recognized her as the woman who had lured Tarzan to the hotel room where, but for her, he would have been killed. The plump Eurasian sitting at the desk and facing her, she had never before seen; and now, for the first time, she saw the face of the man who had seized her, and recognized him as the hotel companion of the woman.

"You are Helen Gregory?" asked the man at the desk.

"Yes. Who are you, and what do you want of me?"

"In the first place," said Atan Thome suavely, "let me assure you that I deeply regret the necessity for this

20

seeming discourtesy. Your brother has something that I want. He would not listen to reason; so there was no other alternative than force."

"My brother? You have not talked with him. He is lost somewhere in the interior."

"Don't lie to me," snapped Thome. "I know your brother well. I was with him on the first expedition. He reached Ashair and made a map of the vicinity, but he would not let me have a copy. He wanted The Father of Diamonds all for himself. It is the route map to Ashair that I want, and I shall hold you until I get it."

Helen laughed in his face. "Your intrigue and melodrama have been quite unnecessary," she said. "All that you would have had to do would have been to ask my father for the map. He would have let you make a copy of it. If this man will come back to the hotel with me, he can copy the map now." She indicated Lal Taask with a nod.

Atan Thome sneered. "You think you can trap me as easily as that?" he demanded.

Helen made a gesture of resignation. "Go on with your play acting if you must," she said, "but it will only waste time and get everyone in trouble. What do you wish me to do?"

"I wish you to write and sign the note I shall dictate to your father," replied Thome. "If that doesn't bring the map, he'll never see you again. I'm leaving for the interior immediately, and I shall take you with me. There are sultans there who will pay a good price for you."

"You must be quite insane to think that you can frighten me with any such wild threats. Those things are not done today, you know, outside of story books. Hurry up and dictate your note; and I'll promise you'll have the map back as quickly as your messenger can bring it, but what assurance have I that you'll keep your end of the bargain and release me?"

"You have only my word," replied Atan Thome, "but I can assure you that I have no wish to harm you. The map is all I wish. Come and sit here while I dictate."

As the sun sank into the west behind tall trees and the shadows lengthened to impart to Loango the semblance of a softened beauty the which the squalid little village did not possess in its own right, the three men discussing the details of the forthcoming safari became suddenly aware of the lateness of the hour.

"I wonder what can be keeping Helen," said Gregory; "it's almost dark. I don't like to have her out so late in a place like this. She should have been back long ago."

"She should never have gone alone," said d'Arnot. "It is not safe here for a woman."

"It is not," agreed Tarzan. "It is never safe where there is civilization."

"I think we should go and look for her," suggested d'Arnot.

"Yes," said Tarzan, "you and I. Mr. Gregory should remain here in case she returns."

"Don't worry, Monsieur Gregory," said d'Arnot, as he and Tarzan left the room; "I'm sure we'll find her safe and sound in some curio shop," but his words were only to reassure Gregory. In his heart was only fear.

As he waited, Gregory tried to convince himself that there was nothing to worry about. He tried to read, but could not fix his mind upon the book. After he had reread one sentence half a dozen times without grasping its sense, he gave up; then he commenced to pace the floor, smoking one cigar after another. He was on the point of starting out himself to search when d'Arnot returned. Gregory looked at him eagerly.

D'Arnot shook his head. "No luck," he said. "I found a number of shop keepers who recalled seeing her, but none who knew when she left the bazaar."

"Where is Tarzan?" asked Gregory.

"He is investigating in the village. If the natives have any knowledge of her, Tarzan will get it out of them. He speaks their language in every sense of the term."

"Here he is now," said Gregory as the ape-man entered the room.

Both men looked up at him questioningly. "You didn't find any trace of her?" asked d'Arnot.

Tarzan shook his head. "None. In the jungle, I could have found her; but here—here, in civilization, a man cannot even find himself."

As he ceased speaking, a window pane crashed behind them; and a missile fell to the floor.

"Mon dieu!" cried d'Arnot. "What is that?"

"Look out!" cried Gregory. "It may be a bomb."

"No," said Tarzan, "it is just a note tied to a stone. Here, let's have a look at it."

"It must be about Helen," said Gregory, taking the note from Tarzan's hand. "Yes, it is. It's from her. Listen! 'Dear Dad: The people who are holding me want Brian's road map to Ashair. They threaten to take me into the interior and sell me if they don't get it. I believe they mean it. Tie the map to stone and throw it out window. Do not follow their messenger, or they will kill me. They promise to return me unharmed as soon as they get the map.' Yes, it's from Helen all right, it's her handwriting. But the fools! They could have had the map for the asking. I only want to find Brian. I'll get the map."

He rose and went into Helen's room, which adjoined his. They heard him strike a match to light a lamp, and then give vent to an exclamation of astonishment that brought the other two men into the room. Gregory was standing before the open upper drawer of the dresser, his face white.

"It's gone," he said. "Some one has stolen the map!"

4

IN A SQUALID room, Wolff sat at a table laboriously wielding a pencil by the light of a kerosene lamp—evidently an unaccustomed task. Every time he made a mark, he wet the tip of the pencil on his tongue, which, in the interims, he chewed. At last his work was completed; and as he eyed it, not without pride, he heaved a sigh and rose.

"I guess this ain't a pretty night's work or anything!"

he soliloquized complacently. "Now they'll both pay—and how!"

* * *

Atan Thome sat alone in the back room of Wong Feng's shop. If he were nervous, the only outward indication of it was the innumerable cigarettes that he smoked. Magra was guarding Helen in the little bedroom adjoining. All three were waiting for the return of Lal Taask with the route map to Ashair. Helen, alone, was positive that it would be forthcoming. The others only hoped.

"Will he let me go when the map comes?" asked Helen.

"He may have to keep you until he can get safely away," replied Magra, "but I'm sure he will let you go then."

"Poor Dad," said the girl. "He'll be worrying terribly. If there's going to be any delay about my release, I'd like to write him another note."

"I'll try and arrange it," said Magra. "I'm very sorry about all this, Miss Gregory," she added after a short silence. "I am really quite as helpless in the matter as you, for reasons which I may not explain; but I may tell you that Atan Thome is obsessed by this desire to possess The Father of Diamonds. At heart he is not a bad man, but I know that he will stop at nothing to realize this one desire; so I hope your father sends the map."

"You really think that he would sell me in the interior if he didn't get it?" demanded the American girl.

"Absolutely," replied Magra. "If he were pressed, he might kill you."

Helen shuddered. "I am glad that he is going to get the map," she said.

Lal Taask opened the door to the back room of Wong Feng's shop, and entered. Atan Thome looked up. "Well?" he inquired.

"They threw it out all right," said Taask; "here it is." He handed the paper to Thome. It was still wrapped around the stone. Thome opened it and read. His face turned dark.

"Is it the map?" asked Lal Taask.

"No," growled Thome. "They say the map has been

24

stolen. They lie! They can't fool Atan Thome, though. They'll never see the girl again, and I'll find Ashair without their map. Listen! There is someone at the door. See who it is."

Lal Taask opened the door a crack and looked out. "It is Wolff," he said.

"Bring him in."

"Nice evening," said Wolff, as he entered the room.

"You didn't come here to tell me that," said Thome. "What is it?"

"What would you give for the route map to Ashair?" asked Wolff.

"Five hundred pounds," replied Thome.

"Not enough. Make it a thousand and a half interest in the diamond, and I'll get the map for you."

"How?"

"I already have it. I stole it from the girl's room."

"Have you got it here?" inquired Thome.

"Yes," replied Wolff, "but don't try any funny business. I left a note with the old woman I'm stopping with. If I'm not back in an hour, she'll take it to the police."

"Let's see the map," said Thome.

Wolff took it from his pocket and held it up in front of the other man, but not near enough for him to snatch it. "Fork over the money, and the map's yours," he said.

Atan Thome drew a thick wallet from an inner pocket and counted out five hundred pounds in Bank of England notes.

"If I had that roll of yours I wouldn't be riskin' my neck lookin' for no Father of Diamonds," said Wolff, as he took the notes and stuffed them in his pocket.

"Are you still going along with the Gregory safari?" asked Thome.

"Sure," replied Wolff; "a poor man's got to work; but I'm goin' to be right with you when you get that diamond. I'm goin' to have my half."

"You can do something more to help me," said Thome, "that will also make the diamond safer for us."

"What's that?" asked Wolff, suspiciously.

"I'm going to have Magra try to go along with the Gregorys. You may be able to help in that. I want her to make friends with them—and make love to Brian Gregory; then if anything goes wrong she'll have some influence with them. I don't want to hang, and neither do you."

"Where do I come in?" asked Wolff.

"You go along and lead them off onto a wrong trail. When they're good and lost, bring Magra up toward Ashair. You've seen the map; so you'll know about where to go. You'll find one of my old camps and wait there for me. Do you understand?"

"Yes."

"And you'll do it?"

"Sure. Why not?"

"All right. Now go along. I'll be seeing you up around Ashair in a couple of months."

After Wolff had left, Thome turned to Lal Taask. "We've got to get out of here tonight," he said. "Go down to the river and bribe the captain of that boat to get up steam and leave for Bonga tonight."

"You are very clever, Master," said Lal Taask. "You will let the young lady go, now that you have the map?"

"No. They didn't give me the map. They may catch up with us; and if they do, it will be just as well to have a hostage."

"Again, Master—you are clever."

*   *   *

It was past midnight when Atan Thome went aboard the river steamer with Lal Taask and Helen. At the gangplank he bid Magra goodby. "Join the Gregory safari by any ruse," he directed. "They may reach Ashair, and I want some one with them I can trust. I must be prepared for any eventuality. If they should beat me to it and get the diamond, you must find some way to communicate with me. You may even get an opportunity to steal the diamond. Watch Wolff. I don't trust him. He has agreed to lead them astray and then bring you up toward Ashair to meet me when I come out. It's a good thing you're in love with Brian Gregory. That will help. Work it for all its worth. I didn't like the idea at first; but when I got to thinking about it, I saw where we could make use of it. Now, goodby; and remember all I have told you."

Taask and Helen had boarded the steamer, the man walking very close to the girl, his pistol pressed against her side, lest she make an outcry.

"I think you are very foolish not to set her free," said Magra.

"I can't now," replied Thome—"not until after you have left the Gregory party. Can't you see?"

"Well, see that no harm comes to her—remember the arm of English law is long." Then Magra turned and walked back into the village.

* * *

After a sleepless night of searching for Helen, Gregory, Tarzan, and d'Arnot were gathered in Gregory's room to formulate their plans.

"I'm afraid there's nothing left to do but notify the authorities," said d'Arnot.

"I suppose you're right," agreed Gregory. "I was so afraid they'd kill her if we notified the police, but now there seems to be nothing else to do."

There was a knock at the door, and the three men looked up. "Come in!" said Gregory.

The door swung slowly open, and Magra stepped into the room.

"You!" exclaimed d'Arnot.

She paid no attention to him, but looked straight at Tarzan. "Brian Gregory," she said, "I have come to help you find your sister."

"What do you know about her? Where is she?" demanded Gregory.

"Atan Thome is taking her into the interior. He left for Bonga on the river boat last night."

"But the boat doesn't sail until today," interrupted d'Arnot.

"Atan Thome bribed the captain to sail last night," Magra explained. "I was to have gone, but—well, why I didn't is immaterial."

"This woman is not to be trusted," said Tarzan.

"You can trust me—always, Brian Gregory." She turned to Gregory. "If you doubt me, keep me with you—as a hostage, perhaps. It is possible that I may be able to help you."

Gregory appeared not to hear her. He seemed stunned. "Both my children," he said. "First Brian, now Helen, sacrificed—and for what?"

"Do not despair, Monsieur Gregory," said d'Arnot. "There must be a way."

"But how?" demanded the older man. "In four days Thome will be in Bonga. The boat will lie there at least one day. Coming back with the current, she will make the return trip in two and a half days, perhaps. Even if we can persuade the captain to return to Bonga immediately Thome will have had six or seven days start of us. He will be far into the interior. He probably has the map that was stolen from Helen's room. We have none. We will not know where to look for him."

"Do not worry on that score," urged d'Arnot. "If Thome is in Africa, Tarzan of the Apes will find him."

"Yes," agreed Gregory, dully, "but what will have happened to my poor girl in the mean time?"

"Wait!" exclaimed d'Arnot. "I have it! There is yet a way. We have a naval seaplane here. I'm sure the authorities will fly us to Bonga. We shall be there when Monseiur Thome lands. What a surprise for Monsieur Thome, eh?"

"Wonderful!" cried Gregory. "How can I ever thank you, Captain?"

Whatever her reaction, Magra's face showed no emotion.

5

AT D'ARNOT'S REQUEST, the authorities were glad to co-operate; and with a delay of only a couple of hours the party was boarding a seaplane anchored in the river. Magra's expression suggested utmost self-satisfaction, as d'Arnot helped her aboard from the native canoe that had brought the party from shore. Wolff, who had never flown, swaggered a bit to hide his inward perturbation. Ogabi's eyes rolled fearfully.

"You see how easily everything was arranged?" exclaimed d'Arnot.

"Thanks to you," replied Gregory.

"How long will it take you to fly to Bonga, Lieutenant?" Tarzan asked the pilot.

"Between two and three hours," replied Lavac.

"It will take the steamer four days, against the current," said d'Arnot. "Atan Thome will find a reception committee waiting at the dock."

As the plane raced up the river into the wind for the take-off, Ogabi closed his eyes and clutched the seat with both hands. When he opened his eyes again, he looked down upon the top of a forest. His face was no longer dark—it was a sickly ashen color.

"This is no place for man, Bwana, in belly of bird," he said to Tarzan.

"But you *are* a man, Ogabi," replied the ape-man; "therefore you are not afraid. Remember that when the storm strikes us."

"What storm?" asked Gregory.

"A storm is coming," replied Tarzan.

"How do you know?" demanded Gregory. "There is not a cloud in the sky."

"Tarzan always knows," said d'Arnot.

How Tarzan had known that a storm was approaching, not even he could have explained. Perhaps he shared with the wild things, by which and among which he had been raised, a peculiar sensitivity beyond the appreciation of men. However that may be, a half hour after he had foretold it, the ship raced into the heart of a tropical storm.

Lavac, who was accustomed to sudden tropical storms, assumed that it covered but a small area and would soon be astern of them. An experienced flier, with a ship equipped with all the instruments necessary for blind flying, he merely increased his elevation and flew into it. The ship rolled and tossed, and Ogabi became a few shades lighter. Wolff clenched his fists until his knuckles were white.

After an hour of it, Lavac turned and motioned d'Arnot

29

to come forward. "It's worse than I'd anticipated, Captain," he said. "Had I better turn back?"

"Got plenty of petrol?" asked d'Arnot.

Lavac nodded. "Yes, sir," he replied.

"Everything else all right?"

"I'm not so sure about the compass."

"Then we wouldn't be any better off flying back than going on," said d'Arnot. "Let's keep on. We're bound to be out of it sooner or later."

For two long hours more Lavac bucked the storm; then the engine spluttered. D'Arnot went forward hurriedly; but before he reached Lavac's side, the engine caught itself again and was purring sweetly. It had been a tense moment for these two. D'Arnot breathed a deep sigh of relief—and then the engine spluttered again and stopped. Lavac worked furiously with a hand pump. D'Arnot turned back toward the cabin.

"Fasten your life belts," he said. "We may have to come down."

"The line's clogged," said Lavac, "and I can't clear it."

D'Arnot glanced at the altimeter. "You've got about three thousand meters," he said. "The average elevation in the vicinity of Bonga is around two hundred. Glide as far as you can, looking for a hole."

"And if I don't find one?" asked Lavac.

D'Arnot shrugged and grimaced. "You're the pilot," he said, "and I understand you're a very good one."

"Thanks," said Lavac. "It will take a *very* good pilot to fly this ship through a forest. I am not that good. Are you going to tell them?"

"What's the use?" asked d'Arnot.

"They might wish to take up some matters with God— matters they have been neglecting to discuss with Him."

"What's wrong?" demanded Wolff. "The engine isn't running."

"You have answered your own question," said d'Arnot, walking back to his seat.

"We're coming down," said Wolff. "He can't see to land. We'll crash."

"Be calm," admonished d'Arnot; "we have not crashed yet."

The passengers sat in tense expectancy as the ship nosed down through storm racked clouds.

"What altitude now, Lavac?" asked d'Arnot.

"Three hundred meters."

"That means we can't be more than three hundred feet from ground at the best," said Gregory. "I remember looking at a map the other day. Nearly all this country back here runs about six hundred feet elevation."

Suddenly Wolff leaped to his feet. "I can't stand it," he cried. "I'm going to jump!"

Tarzan seized him and threw him back into his seat. "Sit still," he said.

"Yes, sit still!" snapped d'Arnot. "Is it not bad enough without that?"

Lavac voiced an exclamation of relief. "We're out of it!" he cried, "and there's water just below us."

A moment later the ship glided to an easy landing on the bosom of a little lake. Only the forest and the jungle were there to welcome it. If there were eyes to see, they remained hidden; and the voices of the jungle were momentarily stilled. The rain beat upon the water, and the wind moaned in the forest. Of these things and of their miraculous escape from death Ogabi was unconscious—he had fainted.

"Do you know where we are, Lieutenant?" asked d'Arnot.

"I haven't the least idea," replied Lavac, "—never saw this lake before."

"Then we are lost?" asked Gregory.

Lavac nodded. "I'm afraid so, sir. My compass wasn't behaving very well; and then, naturally, we must have been blown way off our course."

"How lonely and depressing it looks," said Magra.

"It is the jungle," breathed Tarzan, almost as one might say, "It is home!"

"How discouraging," said Gregory. "Just when it seemed certain that we had overcome every obstacle and found a way to circumvent Thome and rescue Helen, this had to happen. Now we are absolutely helpless. We shall never reach her now, poor child."

"*Non! Non!* my dear Monsieur Gregory, you must not give up," said d'Arnot. "This is only a temporary delay.

31

Lieutenant Lavac will have that fuel line cleared in no time, and as soon as the weather lifts we'll take off again. We have plenty of time. Thome will not reach Bonga for three days yet. As soon as the weather clears, the lieutenant can find Bonga even with no compass at all."

Lavac worked on the fuel line for half an hour; then he called d'Arnot. "The line was not clogged, sir," he said. He looked worried.

"Then what was the trouble?" demanded d'Arnot.

"We are out of fuel. The tank must have been leaking badly, as we had a full load when we left."

"But the reserve tank—what of that?" demanded d'Arnot.

"It was the reserve tank that leaked, and we have emptied the other."

D'Arnot shook his head. "That poor little girl!" he said.

6

OGABI WAS SINGING as he grilled antelope steaks over a fire beside which lay the carcass of the animal. Ogabi's spirits had been rising for four days, for now he was four marches away from that horrible bird thing, in the belly of which he had almost ridden to his death. He had been very fearful that the white men would decide to return to it and fly again. If they had, however, he should have run away into the jungle and hidden. Five white men sat around the fire watching him.

"Pretty well convinced you know where we are now, Tarzan?" asked d'Arnot.

"Yes. I'm quite certain that we are east of Bonga and a little south. That buck I killed ranges in that district."

"Thome probably left Bonga today," said Gregory. "By the time we reach Bonga he'll be many marches ahead of us. We'll never overtake him."

"We don't have to go to Bonga," said Tarzan. "We

can strike out directly northeast and cut his trail; then we can follow on faster than he can travel—boys with packs will slow him down. We're not handicapped by anything like that."

"You mean we can travel without porters or provisions?" demanded Gregory.

"We have been for the last four days," Tarzan reminded him. He looked quickly about the camp. "Where's Magra?" he asked. "I told her not to leave camp. This is lion country; and, if I'm right about the location, it's also cannibal country."

Magra had not meant to go far from the camp; but the forest was intriguing, and it seemed so quiet and peaceful. She walked slowly, enjoying the blooms, watching the birds. She stopped before a lovely orchid, which, like some beautiful woman, sucked the life blood from the giant that supported it. Presently she recalled Tarzan's injunction, and turned to retrace her steps to camp. She did not see the great lion behind her which had caught her scent and was stalking her on silent, padded feet.

The men in the camp saw Tarzan rise to his feet, his head up, his nostrils quivering; then, to their amazement, they saw him run a few steps, swing into a tree, and disappear. They did not know that Usha, the wind, had brought the acrid scent spoor of Numa, the lion, to the sensitive nostrils of the ape-man, and that mingled with it was the delicate scent of the perfume that Magra loved, revealing to him an impending tragedy and sending him into the trees in the hope that he would reach the scene in time.

As Magra walked toward camp, an angry snarl from the king of beasts brought her suddenly about to awareness of the danger that confronted her. Instantly she realized the hopelessness of her situation and the futility of calling for help that could not reach her in time to prevent the inevitable. With her accustomed courage, she resigned herself to death; but even with death staring her in the face, she could scarcely restrain an involuntary exclamation of admiration for the magnificence of the great beast facing her. His size, his majestic bearing, the sheer ferocity of his snarling mien thrilled every fiber of her being. She did not want to die, but she felt that there could be no more noble death than beneath the mighty fangs and talons of the king of beasts.

Now the lion was creeping toward her, belly to ground, the end of his tail twitching nervously. Just for a yard or so he came thus; then he rose, but still crouching a little as he advanced. Suddenly, with a mighty roar, he charged; and at the same instant a man leaped from a tree above full upon his back.

"Brian!" she cried, with a gasp of astonishment.

The man clung to the back of the carnivore, his growls mingling with those of the great cat, as he drove his hunting knife again and again into the tawny side of the leaping, striking beast. Thrilled and horrified, Magra watched, fascinated, until the pierced heart ceased forever, and the great beast died. Then Magra had reason to shudder in real horror, as the Lord of the Jungle placed a foot upon the carcass of his kill and voiced the victory cry of the bull ape. Every fiber of the girl's body vibrated to a new thrill as she watched the man she now knew was not Brian Gregory.

As the uncanny cry broke the stillness of the jungle, Wolff, Gregory, and Lavac sprang to their feet. Wolff seized his rifle. "My God!" he cried. "What was that?"

"Tarzan has a made a kill," said d'Arnot.

"The Big Bwana has killed Simba," said Ogabi. "Are the white men deaf that they did not hear Simba roar?"

"Sure I heard it," said Wolff; "but that wild man never killed no lion—he had nothin' but a knife. I'd better go out there an' look after him." Carrying his rifle, he started in the direction of the sound that had startled them, Gregory and Lavac following. "That yell was when the lion got *him*," said Wolff. "He's deader'n a smelt right now."

"He doesn't look very dead to me," said Lavac, as Tarzan and Magra came into view.

"I'm afraid I was so out of breath that I didn't—well, thank is a most inadequate word under the circumstance; but I can't think of another—thank you for saving my life. How silly and banal that sounds, but you know what I'm trying to say. You were wonderful, and a little terrifying, too; but I know now that you are not Brian Gregory. He could not have killed the lion as you did.

34

No other man in the world could have done it." She paused. "Until a few minutes ago, I thought that I loved Brian."

The implication of Magra's words and tone was quite apparent, yet Tarzan elected to ignore it. "We shall do our best to find him," he said, "not only on Mr. Gregory's account but on yours."

Magra shrugged. She was rebuffed, but she could bide her time. "And the diamond?" she asked.

"I'm not interested in that," said Tarzan.

* * *

A well equipped safari moved toward the northeast ten marches out of Bonga. A girl and two men were the only whites, but the porters seemed to be carrying enough equipment and provisions for two or three times that number.

"Rather clever of me," said one of the men to the girl, "taking your father's safari. It will take him a week or longer to get another one together and equip it. By that time we'll be so far ahead that he'll never overtake us. I should like to see his face when he reaches Bonga and learns the truth."

"You are about as clever as the late Mr. Dillinger and Baby Face Nelson," replied Helen, "and you'll end up the same way."

"Who were they?" demanded Thome.

"They were kidnapers and murderers who were also addicted to grand larceny. If you were not a fool, you'd turn me loose and send me back to Bonga. You have the map. I can be of no further use to you. Until I am returned safely to him, my father will never give up until he finds you. I can't see why you want to hold me any longer."

"Perhaps I have taken a liking to you, my dear," replied Thome.

The girl shuddered at the implication of the man's words. All the rest of the day she plodded on in silence waiting always for a chance to escape, but either Atan Thome or Lal Taask was always at her side. She was spent and weary when they finally made camp, but much of her weariness was from nervous exhaustion—all day long the words of Atan Thome had preyed upon her mind.

After the evening meal, she went to her tent, which had been pitched across the camp from that occupied by Thome, for the man knew that while she might attempt to escape by day, she would not dare to venture the dangers of the forest by night.

Thome and Taask stood talking before the former's tent, Thome's eyes upon the girl entering hers. The two men had been talking, and Lal Taask was watching the other intently.

"You are my master, Atan Thome," he said; "but out of loyalty, your servant must warn you. The girl is white, and the arm of the white man's power is long. Into the depth of the jungle or to the frozen wastes of the poles it would reach and drag you back to an accounting."

"Mind your own affairs," snapped Thome. "I mean the girl no harm."

"I am glad to hear you say that. I do not want the white man's anger upon me. If you are wise you will do as the girl suggested. Send her back to Bonga tomorrow."

Atan Thome thought a moment; then he nodded. "Perhaps you are right," he said. "She shall go back to Bonga tomorrow, if she wishes."

The two men separated, each going to his own tent; and silence fell upon the sleeping camp, a single askari, nodding beside the beast fire, the only suggestion of life within the rude boma that had been thrown up against the intrusion of predatory beasts.

Presently Atan Thome emerged from his tent. His eyes swept the camp. Only the askari was in evidence. At sight of Thome, he simulated an alertness which was, considering the hour and his inclinations, anachronistic; but he was sufficiently aroused to watch the white man creep silently across the camp; and when he understood Atan Thome's evident goal, he grinned. In the distance, a lion roared. This and the love note of the cicada alone broke the silence of the night.

Sleepless from nervous apprehension, Helen's mind was filled with dread and misgiving. The altered attitude of Atan Thome worried her. Every slightest sound bore a menace to her expectant ears. Finally she rose from her couch and looked out through the flap of her tent. Her heart sank as she saw Atan Thome creeping toward her.

Again a lion roared out of the mysterious void of blackness that was the jungle night, but a far greater menace lay in the oily man who parted the flaps at the front of the girl's tent. An aura of repulsiveness surrounded Thome. The girl had always sensed it, feeling in his presence as one might in the presence of a cobra.

Atan Thome pushed the curtains aside and stepped into the tent. The ingratiating, oily smile upon his lips vanished as he discovered that it was vacant. He did not know that the girl had crawled beneath the back wall but a moment before he had entered. For all he knew she might have been gone an hour or more; but he was sure that she must be somewhere about the camp, for he could not imagine that she would have dared the dangers of the jungle night to escape him. Yet this was what she had done.

Frightened, she groped through the darkness which was only partly moderated by the newly risen moon. Again the roar of a hunting lion reverberated through the forest, nearer now; and her heart sank. Yet she steeled herself and stumbled on, more terrified by thoughts of the man behind her than of the lion ahead. She hoped the beast would continue to roar, for in this way she could always locate its position. If it stopped roaring, that might mean that it had caught her scent and was stalking her.

By accident she had stumbled upon a game trail, and this she followed. She thought that it was the back trail toward Bonga, but it was not. It ran in a more southerly direction, which was, perhaps, just as well for her, as the lion was on the Bonga trail; and the sound of its roars receded as she stumbled on through the forest.

After a night of terror, the girl came to an open plain during the early morning. When she saw it, she knew that she had missed the trail to Bonga, for the safari had crossed no plain like this on its trek from the river town. She realized that she was lost, and now she had no plan other than to escape from Thome. Her future, her life lay in the palm of a capricious Fate. How, in this savage land, it could be other than a cruel Fate, she could not imagine; yet she must carry on—and hope.

She was so glad to be out of the forest that she struck out across the plain toward a range of low hills, ignoring the fact that while the forest might be gloomy and depressing, it offered her concealment and escape from many dangers among the branches of its trees. Behind her lay Thome and the memory of the hunting lion. It was well for her peace of mind that she did not know what lay just ahead.

7

CHEMUNGO, SON of Mpingu, Chief of the Buiroos, was hunting with three other warriors for a man-eater which had been terrorizing the villages of his people. They had tracked him through the hills to the edge of a plain beyond which lay a forest; but when they reached a low elevation from which they could survey the plain, they discovered other quarry than that for which they were hunting.

"A white woman," said Chemungo; "we shall take her to my father."

"Wait," counselled a companion; "there will be white men with guns."

"We can wait and see," agreed Chemungo, "for she comes this way. Perhaps there are no white men."

"White women do not come here without white men," insisted the other warrior.

"She may have wandered away from camp and become lost," argued Chemungo; "these white women are very helpless and very stupid. See, she has no weapons; so she is not hunting; therefore she must be lost."

"Perhaps Chemungo is right," admitted the other.

They waited until Helen was well out into the plain; then Chemungo, leaping to his feet, signalled the others to follow him; and the three ran toward the white girl, shouting and waving their spears.

So sudden and so unexpected was the appearance of this new menace that, for a moment, Helen stood paralyzed by terror, almost regretting that she had left either Thome or the lion; then she turned and fled back toward the forest.

Lithe, athletic, the girl seemed in a fair way to outdistance her pursuers. She felt that if she could reach the forest before they overtook her, she might elude them entirely. Behind her, the cries of Chemungo and his fellows were angry cries now, threatening cries, as they redoubled their efforts to overtake their quarry. Terror lent wings to the girl's flying feet; and the warriors, burdened by their spears and shields, were falling behind. Helen, glancing over her shoulder, felt that escape was almost assured, when her retreat was suddenly cut off by the appearance of a great lion which was emerging from the forest directly in front of her. It was the man-eater.

The pursuing warriors redoubled their shouting; and the lion, confused, paused momentarily. Now, indeed was the girl faced by a major dilemma, either horn of which would prove fatal. In an attempt to escape both, she turned to the right—a brave but futile gesture of self-preservation. The moving quarry attracted the lion, which started in pursuit, while the warriors, apparently unafraid, raced to intercept him. They might have succeeded had not Helen tripped and fallen.

As the girl fell, the lion charged and sprang upon her prostrate form; but the shouts of the warriors and their proximity attracted his snarling attention before he had mauled her; and as the four closed in upon him, Chemungo cast his spear. It seemed an act of temerity rather than of courage; but these were warriors of a famous lion-hunting clan, well versed in the technique of their dangerous sport.

Chemungo's spear drove deep into the body of the lion; and, simultaneously, those of two of his companions; the fourth warrior held his weapon in reverse. Roaring horribly, the lion abandoned the girl and charged Chemungo, who threw himself backward upon the ground, his entire body covered by his great shield, while the other warriors danced around them, yelling at the top of their lungs, irritating and confusing the lion; and the fourth warrior awaited his opportunity to drive home the lethal thrust. It came presently, and the lion fell with the spear through his savage heart.

Then Chemungo leaped up and dragged the hapless girl to her feet. She was too stunned by the frightful ordeal through which she had passed to feel either fear or relief. She was alive! Later she was to wonder if it would not have been better had she died.

For hours they dragged her roughly across the plain and through hills to another valley and a village of thatched huts surrounded by a palisade; and as they dragged her through the village street, angry women surrounded them, striking at the girl and spitting upon her. She showed no fear, but half smiled as she likened them to a roomful of envious old women in some civilized city, who might have done likewise but for their inhibitions.

Chemungo took her before his father, Mpingu, the chief. "She was alone," said Chemungo. "No white man can ever know what we do with her. The women wish her killed at once."

"I am chief," snapped Mpingu. "We shall kill her tonight," he added hastily, as he caught the eye of one of his wives. "Tonight we shall dance—and feast."

*   *   *

The Gregory safari debouched from a forest at the edge of a plain which stretched before them, tree dotted, to the foot of a cone-shaped hill. "I know where we are now," said Tarzan, pointing at the hill. "We'll have to travel north and west to reach Bonga."

"If we had grub and porters we wouldn't have to go back," volunteered Wolff.

"We've got to go back to Bonga to get on Thome's trail and find Helen," said Gregory. "If we only had the map, we'd be all right on that score."

"We don't need no map," said Wolff. "I know the way to Ashair."

"That's odd," commented Tarzan. "Back in Loango you said you didn't know the way."

"Well, I know it now," growled Wolff, "and if Gregory

wants to pay me a thousand pounds and cut me in on the diamond, fifty-fifty, I'll take him to Ashair."

"I think you are a crook," said the ape-man, "but if Gregory wants to pay you, I'll take him through without porters."

Catching Tarzan entirely off his guard, and without warning, Wolff knocked the ape-man down. "There can't no damn monkey-man call me a crook," he cried, whipping his pistol from its holster; but before he could fire, Magra seized his arm.

"If I were you, Monsieur Wolff," said d'Arnot, "I should run. I should run very fast—before Tarzan gets up."

But Tarzan was already up; and before Wolff could escape, he seized him by the throat and belt and lifted him high above his head, as though to hurl him to the ground.

"Don't kill him, Tarzan!" cried Gregory, stepping forward. "He is the only man who can lead us to Ashair. I will pay him what he asks. He can have the diamond, if there is one. All I want is to find my daughter and my son. Thome is on his way to Ashair. If Helen is with him, Wolff offers our only hope of rescuing her."

"As you wish," said the ape-man, dropping Wolff upon the ground.

The safari crossed the plain and, skirting the foot of the cone-shaped hill, entered a forest, where camp was made beside a small stream. It was a most primitive camp, as they had no equipment—just rude shelters, a makeshift boma, and a fire. Magra, being the only woman, fared best. Hers was the largest and best constructed shelter, the shelters of the men encircling it for protection. As she stood before it, Wolff passed; and she stopped him. It was the first opportunity she had had to speak to him alone since his altercation with Tarzan.

"Wolff, you *are* a scoundrel," she said. "You promised Atan Thome you'd lead Gregory off the trail. Now you've sold out to him and promised to lead him to Ashair. When I tell Atan Thome that—" She shrugged. "But you do not know Atan Thome as well as I."

"Perhaps you will not tell Atan Thome anything," replied Wolff, meaningly.

"Don't threaten me," warned the girl. "I'm not afraid

of you. Either of two men would kill you if I said the word. Tarzan would wring your neck openly. Thome would have some one stick a knife in your back."

"He might do the same to you, if I told him you were in love with the monkey-man," shot back Wolff; and Magra flushed.

"Don't be a fool," she said. "I have to keep on the good side of these people; and if you had even a semblance of good sense, you'd do the same."

"I don't want to have nothing to do with that monkey-man," growled Wolff. "Me and him ain't in the same class."

"That's obvious," said Magra.

"But with me and you it's different," continued Wolff, ignoring the implication. "We ought to be more friendly. Don't you know we could have a swell time if you'd loosen up a bit? I ain't such a bad fellow when you gets to know me."

"I'm glad to hear that. I was afraid you were."

Wolff knitted his brows. He was trying to digest this when his attention was attracted to Tarzan. "There goes the monkey-man," he said. "Look at him swingin' through the trees. You can't tell *me* he ain't half monkey."

Magra, tiring of Wolff, walked toward d'Arnot just as Gregory came up. "Where's Tarzan going?" asked the latter.

"To reconnoiter for a native village," replied the Frenchman, "on the chance we can get some supplies and a few 'boys'—askaris and porters, and, perhaps, a cook. That would give Tarzan a chance to go on ahead and search for your daughter."

As the Lord of the Jungle swung through the trees in search of some indication of the presence of native habitation his active mind reviewed the events of the past several weeks. He knew that three scoundrels were pitted against him—Thome, Taask, and Wolff. He could cope with them, but could he cope with Magra? He could not understand the girl. Twice she had saved him from the bullets of would-be assassins, yet he knew that she was an associate, perhaps an accomplice, of Thome. The first time it might have been because she had thought him to be Brian Gregory, but now she knew better. It was all quite beyond him. With a shrug, he dismissed the whole matter from his mind, content to know that he was forewarned and, consequently, on guard.

The day was coming to a close as Tarzan gave up the search for a native village and decided to return to camp. Suddenly he stood erect upon a branch of a great tree, head up, statuesque, alert, listening. A vagrant breeze had brought to his nostrils the scent of Wappi, the antelope, suggesting that he take meat back to camp; but as he prepared to stalk his prey, the booming of distant native drums came faintly to his ears.

8

A S NIGHT FELL, Helen, lying bound in a filthy hut, heard the booming of drums in the village street outside. Eerie and menacing they sounded, mysterious, threatening. She felt that they were beating for her —a savage, insistent dirge, foretelling death. She wondered what form it would take, when it would come to her. She felt that she might almost welcome it as an escape from the terror that engulfed her. Presently, warriors came and jerked her roughly to her feet after removing the bonds that confined her ankles; then they dragged her out into the village street before the hut of Mpingu, the chief, and tied her to a stake, while around her milled screaming women and shouting warriors. In the glare of the cooking fires the whole scene seemed to the doomed girl the horrible phantasmagoria of some hideous nightmare from which she must awaken. It was all too fantastic to be real, but when a spear point pierced her flesh and warm blood flowed she knew she did not dream.

*   *   *

A well equipped safari lay in an ordered camp. Porters

and askaris squatted around tiny cook fires; and before the central beast fire, two men who were not natives talked with Mbuli, the headman, while faintly from afar came the sullen sound of native drums.

"They are at it," said Atan Thome. "Mbuli tells me this is cannibal country and that we had better get out quickly. Tomorrow we'll make a long trek toward Ashair. The girl is lost. The drums may be for her."

"Her blood is on your head, master," said Lal Taask.

"Shut up," snapped Thome. "She is a fool. She might have lived happily and enjoyed the fruits of The Father of Diamonds."

Lal Taask shook his head. "The ways of women are beyond the comprehension of even thou, master. She was very young and very beautiful; she loved life; and you took it from her. I warned you, but you would not heed. Her blood is on your head."

Atan Thome turned irritably away, but the drums followed him to his tent and would give him no rest.

* * *

"The drums!" said d'Arnot. "I do not like them; so often they spell death for some poor devil. The first time I heard them, I was tied to a stake; and a lot of painted devils were dancing around me pricking me with spears. They don't quite kill you at first, they just torture you and let you live as long as possible so that you may suffer more, for your suffering is their pleasure."

"But how did you escape?" asked Lavac.

"Tarzan came," said d'Arnot.

"He has not returned," said Magra. "I am afraid for him. Perhaps the drums are for him."

"Do you suppose they could have gotten him?" asked Gregory.

"No such luck," snarled Wolff. "The damn monkey has as many lives as a cat."

D'Arnot turned angrily away; and Gregory, Lavac, and Magra followed him, leaving Wolff alone, listening to the beating of the distant drums.

* * *

The drums had carried their message to Tarzan. They told him of impending torture and sacrifice and death. The lives of strangers meant nothing to the ape-man, who, all his life, had lived with death. It was something that came to all creatures. He had no fear of it, he who feared nothing. To avoid it was a game that added zest to life. To pit his courage, his strength, his agility, his cunning against Death, and win—there was the satisfaction. Some day Death would win, but to that day Tarzan gave no thought. He could fight or he could run away; and in either event preserve his self-respect, for only a fool throws his life away uselessly; and Tarzan had no respect for fools; but if the stake warranted it, he could lightly accept the gravest risks.

As he heard the drums against the new night, he thought less of their sinister portent than of the fact that they would guide him to a native village where, perhaps, he might obtain porters later. First, however, he must reconnoiter and investigate to learn the temper of the natives. If they were fierce and warlike, he must avoid their country, leading his little party around it; and the message of the drums suggested that this would be the case.

As the radio beam guides the flyer, the drums of the Buiroos guided Tarzan as he swung through the trees toward their village. He moved swiftly, anticipating a sport he had enjoyed many times in the course of his savage existence—that of frustrating the Gomangani in the exercise of weird rites of torture and death. The drums told him that a victim was to die, but that death had not as yet been meted out. Who the victim was, was of no importance to the ape-man. All that mattered was the sport of cheating the torturers of the final accomplishment of their aims. Perhaps he would arrive in time, perhaps not. Also, if he did arrive in time, he might fail to accomplish his design. It was these factors that lent interest to the savage game that Tarzan loved to play.

* * *

As Tarzan neared the village of Mpingu, the chief,

45

Atan Thome and Lal Taask sat smoking beside the fire that burned brightly in their camp as a discourager of predatory felines.

"Curse those drums!" snapped Lal Taask. "They give me the creeps; they have my nerves on edge."

"Tomorrow night we shall not hear them," said Atan Thome, "for then we shall be a long way on the trail to Ashair—to Ashair and The Father of Diamonds."

"Wolff will have difficulty catching up with us," said Lal Taask, "and if we come back from Ashair by another route, he will never catch up with us."

"You forget Magra," said Thome.

"No," replied Taask; "I do not forget Magra. She will find her way to Paris as the homing pigeon finds its cote. We shall see her there."

"You underestimate Wolff's cupidity," said Thome. "He will come through for his half of the diamond. Never fear."

"And get this!" Lal Taask touched his knife.

"You are psychic," laughed Thome.

"Those drums!" growled Lal Taask.

* * *

"Those drums!" exclaimed Magra. "Did you ever hear anything so horribly insistent?"

"A radio fan's nightmare," said Gregory; "a boring broadcast that one can't dial out."

"I am so worried about Tarzan," said Magra, "out there all alone in that awful forest."

"I wouldn't worry too much about him," d'Arnot reassured her; "he has spent his life in awful forests, and has a way of taking care of himself."

Wolff grunted. "We don't need him nohow. I can take you to Ashair. We'd be well rid of the monkey-man."

"I've heard about all of that that I care to, Wolff," said d'Arnot. "Tarzan is our only hope either of reaching Ashair or getting out of this country alive. You stick to your hunting job. Even at that you haven't been doing so well. Tarzan has brought in all the meat we've had so far."

"Listen!" exclaimed Lava. "The drums! They've stopped."

The howling pack circled the helpless girl. Now and then a spear point touched her lightly, and involuntarily her flesh recoiled. Later the torture might be more excruciating, or some maddened savage, driven to frenzy by the excitement of the dance, might plunge his spear through her heart and with unintentional mercy deliver her from further suffering.

As Tarzan reached the edge of the clearing where lay the village of Mpingu, the chief, he dropped to the ground and ran swiftly toward the palisade. This side of the village was in darkness, and he knew that all the tribesmen would be gathered around the great fire that lighted the foliage of the trees that grew within the village. He would not be seen, and what slight noise he might make would be drowned by the throbbing of the drums.

With the agility of Sheeta, the panther, he scaled the palisade and dropped down into the shadow of the huts beyond; then he crept silently toward a great tree which overhung the hut of the chief and commanded a view of the main street of the village, where the fire burned and the dancers leaped and howled. Swinging up among the branches, he crossed to the other side of the tree and looked down upon the scene of savagery below. It was almost with a sense of shock that he recognized the victim at the stake. He saw the horde of armed warriors incited to frenzy by the drums, the dancing, the lust for human flesh. He fitted an arrow to his bow.

As one of the dancing savages, carried away by the excitement of the moment, paused before the girl and raised his short spear above his head to drive it through her heart a sudden hush fell upon the expectant assemblage; and Helen closed her eyes. The end had come! She breathed a silent prayer. The ominous hush was broken only by the increased madness of the drums; then came a scream of mortal agony.

The assurance of the savages vanished, as an arrow, mysteriously sped, pierced the heart of the executioner. It was then that the drums stopped.

At the scream of the stricken warrior, Helen opened

47

her eyes. A man lay dead at her feet, and consternation was written on the faces of the savage Buiroos. She saw one, braver than the rest, creeping toward her with a long knife ready in his hand; then a weird and uncanny cry rang out from somewhere above her, as Tarzan of the Apes rose to his full height; and, raising his face to Goro, the Moon, voiced the hideous victory cry of the bull ape that had made a kill. Louder than the drums had been, it carried far out into the night.

*   *   *

"Yes," said d'Arnot, "the drums have stopped—they have probably made the kill. Some poor thing has found relief from torture."

"Oh, what if it were Tarzan!" cried Magra; and as she spoke an eerie scream and wafted faintly across the still African night.

"Mon Dieu!" exlaimed Lavac.

"It is Tarzan who has made a kill," said d'Arnot.

*   *   *

"By the beard of the prophet!" exclaimed Lal Taask. "What a hideous sound!"

"It is Africa, Lal Taask," said Atan Thome, "and that was the victory cry of a bull ape. I have heard it before, on the Congo."

"It was far away," said Lal Taask.

"Still, it was too close for comfort," replied Atan Thome. "We shall break camp very early in the morning."

"But why should we fear apes?" demanded Lal Taask.

"It is not the apes I fear," explained Atan Thome. "I said that that noise was the victory cry of a bull ape, but I am not so sure. I have been talking with Mbuli. Perhaps the man we thought was Brian Gregory was not Brian Gregory at all. I asked Mbuli if he ever heard of a white man called Tarzan. He said that he had; that some thought that he was a demon, and that all who did wrong, feared him. When he kills, Mbuli says, he gives the kill cry of the bull ape. If what we heard was not a bull ape, it was Tarzan; and that means that he is looking for us and is far too close for comfort."

"I do not wish to see that man again," said Lal Taask.

* * *

As the bloodcurdling cry crashed through the silence of the night, the warrior who had been creeping up on Helen straightened up and stepped back, frightened. The others, terror stricken, shrank from the menace of the fearsome sound; then Tarzan spoke.

"The demon of the forest comes for the white memsahib," he said. "Beware!" And as he spoke he dropped to the ground near the stake, trusting, by the very boldness of his move, to overawe the savages for the few moments it would take to free Helen and escape; but he had reckoned without knowing of the courage of Chemungo, son of Mpingu, standing ready with his knife.

"Chemungo, son of Mpingu, is not afraid of the demon of the forest," he shouted, as he sprang forward with upraised knife; and as the last of Helen's bonds fell away, Tarzan slipped his own knife back into its sheath and turned to meet the chief's son, the challenging "Kre-e-gah!" on his lips. With bare hands he faced the infuriated warrior.

As Chemungo closed with upraised knife hand ready to strike, Tarzan seized him by the right wrist and at the belly and swung him high above his head as lightly as though he had been a child. The knife dropped from Chemungo's hand as the steel thews of the ape-man closed with viselike grip upon his wrist.

Helen Gregory, almost unable to believe her own senses, looked with astonishment upon this amazing man who dared face a whole cannibal village alone; and could see no hope but that two lives instead of one must now be sacrificed. It was a brave, a glorious gesture that Tarzan had made; but how pathetically futile!

"Open the gates!" he commanded the astounded throng, "or Chemungo, son of Mpingu, dies."

The villagers hesitated. Some of the warriors grumbled. Would they obey, or would they charge?

C OME!" SAID TARZAN to Helen, and without waiting for any reply from the savages, he started toward the gate, still carrying Chemungo above his head; and Helen walked at his side.

Some of the warriors started to close upon them. It was a tense moment, fraught with danger. Then Mpingu spoke. "Wait!" he commanded his warriors, and then to Tarzan, "If I open the gates will you set Chemungo free, unharmed?"

"When I have gone a spear throw beyond the gates, I will free him," replied the ape man.

"How do I know that you will do that?" demanded Mpingu. "How do I know that you will not take him into the forest and kill him?"

"You know only what I tell you, Gomangani," replied Tarzan. "I tell you that if you open the gates and let us go out in safety, I shall free him. If you do not open the gates, I shall kill him now."

"Open the gates!" commanded Mpingu.

And so Tarzan and Helen passed in safety out of the village of the cannibals and into the black African night; and beyond the gates Tarzan liberated Chemungo.

"How did you happen to fall into the hands of those people?" Tarzan asked Helen, as they set their faces toward the Gregory camp.

"I escaped from Atan Thome's camp last night and tried to make my way back to Bonga; but I got lost, and then they got me. There was a lion, too. He had me down, but they killed him. I have had a horrible time. I couldn't believe my eyes when I saw you. How in the world did you happen to be here?"

He told her of the events that had led up to his discovery of her in the cannibal village.

"It will be good to see Dad again," she said; "I can scarcely believe it even now. And Captain d'Arnot came, too—how wonderful!"

"Yes," he said, "he is with us, and Lavac, the pilot who flew us out of Loango, and Wolff, and Magra."

She shook her head. "I don't know about Magra," she said. "I can't understand her. She seemed very sorry for me in Loango after I was kidnaped, but she couldn't do anything for me. I think she was afraid of Atan Thome. Yet she is linked with him in some way. She is a very mysterious woman."

"She will bear watching," said Tarzan; "both she and Wolff."

*   *   *

The sun was an hour high as Magra came from her shelter and joined the others around the fire where Obagi was grilling the remainder of the antelope. Her eyes were heavy, and she appeared unrested. They bade her good morning, but their faces suggested that it seemed anything but a good morning. She looked quickly about, as though searching for some one.

"Tarzan did not return?" she asked.

"No," said Gregory.

"This suspense is unbearable," she said. "I scarcely closed my eyes all night, worrying about him."

"And think of Monsieur Gregory and me, Ma'moiselle," d'Arnot reminded her. "Not only have we to worry about Tarzan, but Helen—Miss Gregory—as well." Gregory shot a quick glance at the Frenchman.

A few minutes later, the others walked away, leaving Magra and d'Arnot alone.

"You are very fond of Miss Gregory, are you not?" asked Magra.

"*Oui,*" admitted d'Arnot. "Who would not be?"

"She is very nice," agreed Magra. "I wish that I might have helped her."

"Helped her? What do you mean?"

"I can't explain; but believe me, no matter what appearances may be or what you may all think of me, I have been helpless. I am bound by the oath of another—an oath

51

I must in honor respect. I am not a free agent. I cannot always do as I wish."

"I shall try to believe," said d'Arnot, "even though I do not understand."

"Look!" cried Magra, suddenly. "Here they are now —both of them! How can it be possible?"

D'Arnot looked up to see Tarzan and Helen approaching the camp; and, with Gregory, he ran forward to meet them. Gregory's eyes filled with tears as he took Helen in his arms, and d'Arnot could not speak. Lavac joined them and was introduced to Helen, after which his eyes never left her when he could look at her unobserved. Only Wolff held back. Sullen and scowling, he remained seated where he had been.

The greetings over, Tarzan and Helen finished what was left of the antelope; and while they ate, Helen recounted her adventures.

"Thome shall pay for this," said Gregory.

"He should die for it," exclaimed d'Arnot.

"I should like to be the one to kill him," muttered Lavac.

Day after day the little party trudged on through forests, across plains, over hills; but never did they strike a sign of Atan Thome's trail. Either Lavac or d'Arnot was constantly at the side of Helen Gregory in a growing rivalry of which only Helen seemed to be unaware, but then one cannot always know of just how much a woman is unaware. She laughed and joked or talked seriously with either of them impartially. D'Arnot was always affable and in high spirits, but Lavac was often moody. Tarzan hunted for the party, as Wolff seemed never to be able to find game. The latter occasionally went off by himself and studied the route map to Ashair. He was the guide.

Early one morning Tarzan told Gregry that he might be away from the safari all that day and possibly the next.

"But why?" asked the latter.

"I'll tell you when I get back," replied the ape-man.

"Shall we wait here for you?"

"As you wish. I'll find you in any event." Then he was gone at the swinging, easy trot with which he covered so much distance on foot.

"Where's Tarzan gone?" asked d'Arnot as he joined Gregory.

The older man shrugged. "I don't know. He wouldn't tell me. Said he might be away a couple of days. I can't imagine why he went."

Wolff joined them then. "Where's the monkey-man gone now?" he asked. "We've got enough meat for two days—all we can carry."

Gregory told him all he knew, and Wolff sneered. "He's ditching you," he said. "Any one could see that. There's no reason for him goin' except that. You won't never see him again."

D'Arnot, usually slow to anger, struck Wolff heavily across the cheek. "I've heard all of that from you I intend to," he said.

Wolff reached for his gun, but d'Arnot had him covered before he could draw. Gregory stepped between them.

"We can't have anything like this," he said. "We've enough troubles without fighting among ourselves."

"I'm sorry, Monsieur Gregory," said d'Arnot, holstering his weapon.

Wolff turned and walked away, muttering to himself.

"What had we better do, Captain?" asked Gregory. "Wait here for Tarzan? or go on?"

"We might as well go on," said d'Arnot. "We might just lose a day or two by staying here."

"But if we go on, Tarzan might not be able to find us," objected Gregory.

D'Arnot laughed. "Even yet, you do not know Tarzan," he said. "You might as well fear to lose yourself on the main street of your native city as think that Tarzan could lose us in two days, anywhere in Africa."

"Very well," said Gregory, "let's go on."

As they moved on behind Wolff, Lavac was walking beside Helen.

"What a deadly experience this would be," he said, "if it were not for—" He hesitated.

"Not for what?" said the girl.

"You," he said.

"Me? I don't understand what you mean."

"That is because you've never been in love," he replied, huskily.

53

Helen laughed. "Oh," she cried, "are you trying to tell me you're in love with me? It must be the altitude."

"You laugh at my love?" he demanded.

"No," she said, "at you. Magra and I are the only women you have seen for weeks. You were bound to have fallen in love with one of us, being a Frenchman; and Magra is so obviously in love with Tarzan that it would have been a waste of time to have fallen in love with her. Please forget it."

"I shall never forget it," said Lavac, "and I shall never give up. I am mad about you, Helen. Please give me something to hope for. I tell you I'm desperate. I won't be responsible for what I may do, if you don't tell me that there may be a little hope for me."

"I'm sorry," she said, seriously, "but I just don't love you. If you are going to act like this, you will make everything even more disagreeable than it already is."

"You are cruel," grumbled Lavac; and for the rest of the day walked moodily alone, nursing his jealousy of d'Arnot.

And there was another who was imbued with thoughts of love that clamored for expression. It was Wolff, and just to be charitable let us call the sentiment that moved him love. He had been leading the safari, but the game trail he was following was too plain to be missed; so he dropped back beside Magra.

"Listen, beautiful," he said. "I'm sorry for what I said the other day. I wouldn't hurt you for nothin'. I know we ain't always hit it off so good, but I'm for you. There ain't nothin' I wouldn't do for you. Why can't we be friends? We could go a long way, if we worked together."

"Meaning what?" asked Magra.

"Meaning I got what it takes to make a woman happy —two strings on that big diamond and £2000 in real money. Think what me and you could do in God's country with all that!"

"With *you?*" she sneered.

"Yes, with me. Ain't I good enough for you?" he demanded.

Magra looked at him, and laughed.

Wolff flushed. "Look here," he said, angrily; "if you think you can treat me like dirt and get away with it, you're all wrong. I just been offerin' to marry you, but I ain't good enough. Well, let me tell you this—I always get what I go after. I'll get you; and I won't have to marry you, neither. You're stuck on that monkey-man; but he can't even see you, and anyway he hasn't got tuppence to rub together."

"A guide belongs at the head of the safari," said Magra; "good-by."

Late in the afternoon Tarzan dropped from the branches of a tree into the midst of the trekking safari, if the six whites and Ogabi could be called a safari. The seven stopped and gathered around him.

"I'm glad you're back," said Gregory. "I'm always worried when you are away."

"I went to look for Thome's trail," said Tarzan, "and I found it."

"Good!" exclaimed Gregory.

"He's a long way ahead of us," continued the ape-man, "thanks to you, Wolff."

"Anyone can make a mistake," growled Wolff.

"You made no mistake," snapped Tarzan. "You have tried, deliberately, to lead us off the trail. We'd be better off without this man, Gregory. You should dismiss him."

"You can't turn me out alone in this country," said Wolff.

"You'd be surprised what Tarzan can do," remarked d'Arnot.

"I think it would be a little too drastic," said Gregory.

Tarzan shrugged. "Very well," he said; "as you will, but we'll dispense with his services as guide from now on."

10

ATAN THOME AND Lal Taask stood at the head of their safari, which had just emerged from a dense forest. At their right ran a quiet river; and before them stretched rough, open country. In the distance, visible above low hills, rose the summit of what appeared to be a huge extinct volcano.

"Look, Lal Taask!" exclaimed Thome. "It is Tuen-Baka. Inside its crater lies Ashair, The Forbidden City."

"And The Father of Diamonds, Master," added Lal Taask.

"Yes, The Father of Diamonds. I wish that Magra were here to see. I wonder where they are. Wolff must be on his way here with her by now. Perhaps we shall meet them when we come out; they could scarcely have overtaken us—we have moved too swiftly."

"If we do not meet them, there will be fewer with whom to divide," suggested Lal Taask.

"I promised her mother," said Thome.

"That was a long time ago; and her mother is dead, and Magra never knew of the promise."

"The memory of her mother never dies," said Thome. "You have been a faithful servitor, Lal Taask. Perhaps I should tell you the story; then you will understand."

"Your servant listens."

"Magra's mother was the only woman I ever loved. The inexorable laws of caste rendered her unobtainable by me. I am a mongrel. She was the daughter of a maharaja. I was trusted in the service of her father; and when the princess married an Englishman, I was sent to England with her in her entourage. While her husband was hunting big game in Africa, he stumbled upon Ashair. For three years he was a prisoner there, undergoing cruelties and torture. At last he managed to escape, and returned home only to die as a result of his experiences. But he brought the story of The Father of Diamonds, and exacted from his wife a promise that she would organize an expedition to return to Ashair and punish those who had treated him so cruelly. The Father of Diamonds was to be the incentive to obtain volunteers; but the map he made became lost, and nothing was ever done. Then the princess died, leaving Magra, who was then ten years old, in my care; for the old maharaja was dead, and his successor would have nothing to do with the daughter of the Englishman. I have always had it in my mind to look for Ashair, and two years ago I made the first attempt. It was then that I learned that Brian Gregory was on a similar quest. He reached Ashair and made a map, though he never actually entered the city. On his second venture, I followed him; but got lost. I met the remnants of his safari coming out. He had disappeared. They refused to give me the map; so I swore to obtain it, and here I am with the map."

"How did you know he made a map?" asked Lal Taask.

"Our safaris met for one night, after his first trip in. I just happened to see him making the map. It is the one I have, or, rather, a copy of it that he sent home in a letter.

"Because Magra's father died because of The Father of Diamonds, a share of it belongs to her; and there is another reason. I am not yet an old man. I see in Magra the reincarnation of the woman I loved. Do you understand, Lal Taask?"

"Yes, master."

Atan Thome sighed. "Perhaps I dream foolish dreams. We shall see, but now we must move on. Come, Mbuli, get the boys going!"

The natives had been whispering among themselves while Thome and Taask talked, now Mbuli came to Atan Thome.

"My people will go no farther, bwana," he said.

"What!" exclaimed Thome. "You must be crazy. I hired you to go to Ashair."

"In Bonga, Ashair was a long way off; and the spirits of my people were brave. Now Bonga is a long way off and Ashair is near. Now they remember that Tuen-Baka is taboo, and they are afraid."

"You are headman," snapped Thome. "You make them come."

"No can do," insisted Mbuli.

"We'll camp here by the river tonight," said Thome. "I'll talk with them. They may feel braver tomorrow. They certainly can't quit on me now."

"Very well, bwana; tomorrow they may feel braver. It would be well to camp here tonight."

Atan Thome and Lal Taask slept well that night, lulled by the soothing murmuring of the river; and Atan Thome dreamed of The Father of Diamonds and Magra. Lal Taask thought that he dreamed when the silence of the night was broken by a sepulchral voice speaking in a strange tongue, but it was no dream.

The sun was high when Atan Thome awoke. He called his boy, but there was no response; then he called again, loudly, peremptorily. He listened. The camp was strangely silent. Rising, he went to the front of the tent and parted the flaps. Except for his tent and Lal Taask's, the camp was deserted. He crossed to Taask's tent and awakened him.

"What is the matter, master?" asked Lal Taask.

"The dogs have deserted us," exclaimed Thome.

Taask leaped to his feet and came out of his tent. "By Allah! They have taken all our provisions and equipment with them. They have left us to die. We must hurry after them. They can't be very far away."

"We shall do nothing of the sort," said Thome. "We're going on!" There was a strange light in his eyes that Lal Taask had never seen there before. "Do you think I have gone through what I have gone through to turn back now because a few cowardly natives are afraid?"

"But, master, we cannot go on alone, just we two," begged Lal Taask.

"Silence!" commanded Thome. "We go on to Ashair —to the Forbidden City and The Father of Diamonds. The Father of Diamonds!" He broke into wild laughter. "Magra shall wear the finest diamonds in the world. We shall be rich, rich beyond the wildest dreams of avarice —she and I—the richest people in the world! I, Atan Thome, the mongrel, shall put the maharajas of India to shame. I shall strew the streets of Paris with gold. I—" He stopped suddenly and pressed a palm to his forehead. "Come!" he said presently in his normal tone. "We'll follow the river up to Ashair."

In silence, Lal Taask followed his master along a narrow trail that paralleled the river. The ground was rough and broken by gullies and ravines, the trail was faint across rocky, barren ground. Near noon they reached the mouth of a narrow gorge with precipitous cliffs on either side, cliffs that towered high above them, dwarfing the two men to Lilliputian proportions. Through the gorge flowed the river, placidly.

"Siva! What a place!" exclaimed Lal Taask. "We can go no farther."

"It is the trail to Ashair," said Thome, pointing. "See it winding along the face of the cliff?"

"That, a trail!" exclaimed Taask. "It is only a scratch that a mountain goat couldn't find footing on."

"Nevertheless, it is the trail that we follow," said Thome.

"Master, it is madness!" cried Lal Taask. "Let us turn back. All the diamonds in the world are not worth the risk. Before we have gone a hundred yards we shall have fallen into the river and drowned."

"Shut up!" snapped Thome, "and follow me."

Clinging precariously to a narrow foot path scratched in the face of the towering cliff, the two men inched their way along the rocky wall. Below them flowed the silent river that rose somewhere in the mystery that lay ahead. A single mis-step would cast them into it. Lal Taask dared not look down. Facing the wall, with arms outspread searching for handholds that were not there, trembling so that he feared his knees would give beneath him and hurl him to death, he followed his master, sweat gushing from every pore.

"We'll never make it," he panted.

"Shut up and come along!" snapped Thome. "If I fall, you may turn back."

"Oh, master, I couldn't even do that. No one could turn around on this hideous trail."

"Then keep coming and quit making such a fuss. You make me nervous."

"And to think you take such risks for a diamond! If it were as big as a house and I had it now, I'd give it to be back in Lahore."

"You are a coward, Lal Taask," snapped Thome.

"I am, master; but it is better to be a live coward than a dead fool."

For two hours the men moved slowly along the narrow foot path until both were on the verge of exhaustion, and even Thome was beginning to regret his temerity; then, as he turned a jutting shoulder in the cliff, he saw a little wooded canyon that broke the face of the mighty escarpment and ran gently down to the river. Down into this canyon the trail led. When they reached it, they threw themselves upon the ground in total exhaustion; and lay there until almost dark.

Finally they aroused themselves and built a fire, for with the coming of night a chill settled upon the canyon. All day they had been without food; and they were famished, but there was nothing for them to eat, and they had to content themselves by filling their bellies with water at the river. For warmth, they huddled close to their little fire.

"Master, this is an evil place," said Lal Taask. "I have a feeling that we are being watched."

"It is the evil within you speaking, fool," growled Thome.

"Allah! Master, look!" faltered Taask. "What is it?" He pointed into the blackness among the trees; and then a sepulchral voice spoke in a strange tongue, and Lal Taask fainted.

11

U NGO, THE KING ape, was hunting with his tribe. They were nervous and irritable, for it was the period of the Dum-Dum; and as yet they had found no victim for the sacrificial dance. Suddenly the shaggy king raised his head and sniffed the air. He growled his disapproval of the evidence that Usha, the wind, brought to his nostrils. The other apes looked at him questioningly.

"Gomangani, tarmangani," he said. "They come"; then he led his people into the underbrush and hid close to the trail.

The little band of men and women who formed the Gregory "safari" followed the plain trail left by Atan Thome's safari, while Tarzan hunted for meat far afield.

"Tarzan must have had difficulty in locating game," said d'Arnot. "I haven't heard his kill-call yet."

"He's marvellous," said Magra. "We'd have starved to death if it hadn't been for him—even with a *hunter* along."

"Well, you can't shoot game where there ain't none," growled Wolff.

"Tarzan never comes back empty handed," said Magra; "and he hasn't any gun, either."

"The other monkeys find food, too," sneered Wolff; "but who wants to be a monkey?"

Ungo was watching them now, as they came in sight along the trail. His close-set, bloodshot eyes blazed with anger; and then suddenly and without warning he charged, and his whole tribe followed him. The little band fell back in dismay. D'Arnot whipped out his pistol and fired; and an ape fell, screaming; then the others were among them, and he could not fire again without endangering his companions. Wolff ran. Lavac and Gregory were both knocked down and bitten. For a few moments all was confusion, so that afterward no one could recall just what happened. The apes were among them and gone again; and when they went, Ungo carried Magra off under one great hairy arm.

Magra struggled to escape until she was exhausted, but the powerful beast that carried her paid little attention to her struggles. Once, annoyed, he cuffed her, almost knocking her insensible; then she ceased, waiting and hoping for some opportunity to escape. She wondered to what awful fate she was being dragged. So man-like was the huge creature, she shuddered as she contemplated what might befall her.

Half carrying her, half dragging her through the woods, with his huge fellows lumbering behind, Ungo, the king ape, bore the girl to a small, natural clearing, a primitive arena where, from time immemorial, the great apes had held their sacrificial dance. There he threw her roughly to the ground, and two females squatted beside her to see that she did not escape.

Back on the trail, the little party, overwhelmed by the tragedy of this misadventure, stood debating what they had best do.

"We could follow them," said d'Arnot; "but we haven't a chance of overtaking them, and if we did, what could we do against them, even though we are armed?"

"But we can't just stand here and do nothing," cried Helen.

"I'll tell you," said d'Arnot. "I'll take Wolff's rifle and

follow them. I may be able to pick off enough of them to frighten the others away if I come up with them after they halt; then, when Tarzan returns, send him after me."

"Here's Tarzàn now," said Helen, as the ape-man came trotting along the trail with the carcass of his kill across his shoulder.

Tarzan found a very disorganized party as he joined them. They were all excited and trying to talk at the same time.

"We never saw them 'til they jumped us," said Lavac.

"They were as big as gorillas," added Helen.

"They were gorillas," put in Wolff.

"They were not gorillas," contradicted d'Arnot; "and anyway, you didn't wait to see what they were."

"The biggest one carried Magra off under his arm," said Gregory.

"They took Magra?" Tarzan looked concerned. "Why didn't you say so in the first place? Which way did they go?"

D'Arnot pointed in the direction in which the apes had made off.

"Keep on this trail until you find a good place to camp," said Tarzan; then he was gone.

As the moon rose slowly over the arena where Magra lay beside a primitive earthen drum upon which three old apes beat with sticks, several of the great shaggy bulls commenced to dance around her. Menacing her with heavy sticks, the bulls leaped and whirled as they circled the frightened girl. Magra had no knowledge of the significance of these rites. She only guessed that she was to die.

The Lord of the Jungle followed the trail of the great apes through the darkness of the forest as unerringly as though he were following a well marked spoor by daylight, followed it by the scent of the anthropoids that clung to the grasses and the foliage of the underbrush, tainting the air with the effluvia of the great bodies. He knew that he should come upon them eventually, but would he be in time?

As the moon rose, the throbbing of the earthen drum directed him toward the arena of the Dum-Dum; so that he could take to the trees and move more swiftly in a direct line. It told him, too, the nature of the danger that threatened Magra. He knew that she still lived, for the drum would be stilled only after her death, when the apes would be fighting over her body and tearing it to pieces. He knew, because he had leaped and danced in the moonlight at many a Dum-Dum when Sheeta, the panther, or Wappi, the antelope, was the sacrificial victim.

The moon was almost at zenith as he neared the arena. When it hung at zenith would be the moment of the kill; and in the arena, the shaggy bulls danced in simulation of the hunt. Magra lay as they had thrown her, exhausted, hopeless, resigned to death, knowing that nothing could save her now.

Goro, the moon, hung upon the verge of the fateful moment, when a tarmangani, naked but for a G string, dropped from an overhanging tree into the arena. With growls and mutterings of rage, the bulls turned upon the intruder who dared thus sacrilegiously to invade the sanctity of their holy of holies. The king ape, crouching, led them.

"I am Ungo," he said. "I kill!"

Tarzan, too, crouched and growled as he advanced to meet the king ape. "I am Tarzan of the Apes," he said in the language of the first-men, the only language he had known for the first twenty years of his life. "I am Tarzan of the Apes, mighty hunter, mighty fighter. I kill!"

One word of the ape-man's challenge Magra had understood—"Tarzan." Astounded, she opened her eyes to see the king ape and Tarzan circling one another, each looking for an opening. What a brave but what a futile gesture the man was making in her defense! He was giving his life for her, and uselessly. What chance had he against the huge, primordial beast?

Suddenly, Tarzan reached out and seized the ape's wrist; then, turning quickly, he hurled the great creature over his shoulder heavily to the ground; but instantly Ungo was on his feet again. Growling and roaring horribly, he charged. This time he would overwhelm the puny man-thing with his great weight, crush him in those mighty arms.

Magra trembled for the man, and she blanched as she saw him meet the charge with growls equally as bestial as those of the ape. Could this growling, snarling beast be the quiet, resourceful man she had come to love? Was he, after all, but a primitive Dr. Jekyll and Mr. Hyde? Spellbound and horrified, she watched.

Swift as Ara, the lightning, is Tarzan; as agile as Sheeta, the panther. Dodging, and ducking beneath Ungo's great flailing arms, he leaped upon the hairy back and locked a full Nelson on the raging ape. As he applied the pressure of his mighty thews, the ape screamed in agony.

"Kreegah!" shouted Tarzan, bearing down a little harder. "Surrender!"

The members of the Gregory party sat around their camp fire listening to the throbbing of the distant drum and waiting in nervous expectancy, for what, they did not know.

"It is the Dum-Dum of the great apes, I think," said d'Arnot. "Tarzan has told me about them. When the full moon hangs at zenith, the bulls kill a victim. It is, perhaps, a rite older than the human race, the tiny germ from which all religious observances have sprung."

"And Tarzan has seen this rite performed?" asked Helen.

"He was raised by the great apes," explained d'Arnot, "and he has danced the dance of death in many a Dum-Dum."

"He has helped to kill men and women and tear them to pieces?" demanded Helen.

"No, no!" cried d'Arnot. "The apes rarely secure a human victim. They did so only once while Tarzan ranged with them, and he saved that one. The victim they prefer is their greatest enemy, the panther."

"And you think the drums are for Magra?" asked Lavac.

"Yes," said d'Arnot, "I fear so."

"I wish I'd gone after her myself," said Wolff. "That guy didn't have no gun."

"He may not have had a gun," said d'Arnot, "but at least he went in the right direction." Wolff lapsed into moody silence. "We all had a chance to do something when the ape first took her," continued d'Arnot; "but, frankly, I was too stunned to think."

"It all happened so quickly," said Gregory. "It was over before I really knew what *had* happened."

"Listen!" exclaimed d'Arnot. "The drums have stopped.

He looked up at the moon. "The moon is at zenith," he said. "Tarzan must have been too late."

"Them gorillas would pull him apart," said Wolff. "If it wasn't for Magra, I'd say good riddance."

"Shut up!" snapped Gregory. "Without Tarzan, we're lost."

As they talked, Tarzan and Ungo battled in the arena; and Magra watched in fearful astonishment. She could scarcely believe her eyes as she saw the great ape helpless in the hands of the man. Ungo was screaming in pain. Slowly, relentlessly, his neck was being broken. At last he could stand it no longer, and bellowed, "Kreegah!" which means "I surrender"; and Tarzan released him and sprang to his feet.

"Tarzan is king!" he cried, facing the other bulls.

He stood there, waiting; but no young bull came forward to dispute the right of kingship with him. They had seen what he had done to Ungo, and they were afraid. Thus, by grace of a custom ages old, Tarzan became king of the tribe.

Magra did not understand. She was still terrified. Springing to her feet, she ran to Tarzan and threw her arms about him, pressing close. "I am afraid," she said. "Now they will kill us both."

Tarzan shook his head. "No," he said; "they will not kill us. They will do whatever I tell them to do, for now I am their king."

12

IN THE LIGHT of early morning, after a night of terror, Atan Thome and Lal Taask started to retrace their steps along the precarious pathway they had so laboriously risked the day before.

"I am glad, master, that you decided to turn back," said Lal Taask.

"Without porters and askaris, it would be madness to attempt to force our way into The Forbidden City," growled

Thome. "We'll return to Bonga and enlist a strong force of men who fear no taboos."

"If we live to get to Bonga," said Lal Taask.

"Cowards invite death," snapped Thome.

"After last night, who would not be a coward in this damnable country?" demanded Taask. "You saw it, didn't you? You heard that voice?"

"Yes," admitted Thome.

"What was it?"

"I don't know."

"It was evil," said Taask. "It breathed of the grave and of Hell. Men cannot prevail against the forces of another world."

"Rot!" ejaculated Thome. "It has some rational and mundane explanation, if we only knew."

"But we don't know. I do not care to know. I shall never return here, if Allah permits me to escape alive."

"Then you will get no share of the diamond," threatened Atan Thome.

"I shall be content with my life," replied Lal Taask.

The two men succeeded in negotiating the return trip in safety, and stood again at last upon level ground near the mouth of the gorge. Lal Taask breathed a sigh of relief, and his spirits rose; but Atan Thome was moody and irritable. He had built his hopes so high that to be turned back at what he believed to be the threshold of success plunged him into despondency. With bowed head, he led the way back over the rough terrain toward their last camp at the edge of the forest.

As they were passing through one of the numerous ravines, they were suddenly confronted by a dozen white warriors who leaped from behind great lava boulders and barred their way. They were stalwart men, wearing white plumes and short tunics on the breasts and backs of which were woven a conventionalized bird. They were armed with spears and knives which hung in scabbards at their hips.

The leader spoke to Thome in a strange tongue; but when he discovered that neither could understand the other, he gave an order to his men who herded Thome and Taask down the ravine to the river, where lay such a craft as may have floated on the Nile in the days of the

66

Pharaohs. It was an open galley, manned by twenty slaves chained to the thwarts.

At the points of spears, Thome and Taask were herded aboard; and when the last of the warriors had stepped across the gunwale, the boat put off and started up stream.

Atan Thome broke into laughter; and Lal Taask looked at him in surprise, as did the warriors near him.

"Why do you laugh, master?" asked Lal Taask, fearfully.

"I laugh," cried Thome, "because after all I shall reach The Forbidden City."

* * *

As Helen came from her shelter early in the morning, she saw d'Arnot sitting beside the embers of the dying beast fire; and she joined him.

"Sentry duty?" she asked.

He nodded. "Yes," he said; "I have been doing sentry duty and a lot of thinking."

"About what, for instance?" she asked.

"About you—us; and what we are going to do," he replied.

"I talked with Father last night, just before I went to bed," she said; "and he has decided to return to Bonga and organize a safari. He doesn't dare go on without Tarzan."

"He is wise," said d'Arnot. "Your life is too precious to risk further." He hesitated, embarrassed. "You don't know what it means to *me*, Helen. I know that this is no time to speak of love; but you must have seen—haven't you?"

"Et tu, Brute!" exclaimed the girl.

"What do you mean?" he demanded.

"Lieutenant Lavac also thinks he is in love with me. Can't you see, Paul, that it is just because I am practically the only girl available—poor Magra was so much in love with Tarzan."

"That is not true with me," he said. "I do not believe it is the explanation as far as Lavac is concerned. He is a fine fellow. I can't blame him for falling in love with you. No, Helen, I'm quite sure of myself. You see, I have taken to losing my appetite and looking at the moon." He laughed. "Those are certain symptoms, you know. Pretty soon I shall take to writing poetry."

"You're a dear," she said. "I'm glad you have a sense of humor. I'm afraid the poor lieutenant hasn't, but then maybe he hasn't had as much experience as you."

"There should be an S.P.C.L.," he said.

"What's that?"

"Society for the Prevention of Cruelty to Lovers."

"Idiot. Wait until you get back where there are lots of girls; then—" She stopped as she glanced across his shoulder. Her face went white, and her eyes were wide with terror.

"Helen! What is it?" he demanded.

"Oh, Paul—the apes have come back!"

D'Arnot turned to see the great beasts lumbering along the trail; then he shouted for Gregory and Lavac. "Name of a name!" he cried an instant later. "Tarzan and Magra are with them!"

"They are prisoners!" exclaimed Helen.

"Non," said d'Arnot; "Tarzan is leading the apes! Was there ever such a man?"

"I'm faint with relief," said Helen. "I never expected to see them again. I'd given them up for lost, especially Magra. It is like seeing a ghost. Why, we even knew the minute that she died last night—when the drumming stopped."

Tarzan and Magra were greeted enthusiastically, and Magra had to tell her story of adventure and rescue. "I know it seems incredible," she added; "but here we are, and here are the apes. If you don't believe me, ask them."

"What are them beggars hangin' 'round for?" demanded Wolff. "We ought to give 'em a few rounds for luck. They got it comin' to 'em for stealin' Magra."

"They are my people," said Tarzan; "they are obeying orders. You shall not harm them."

"They may be your people," grumbled Wolff; "but they ain't mine, me not bein' no monkey."

"They are going along with us," said Tarzan to Gregory. "If you'll all keep away from them and do not touch them, they won't harm you; and they may be helpful to us in many ways. You see, this species of anthropoid ape is

68

highly intelligent. They have developed at least the rudiments of co-operation, the lack of which among the lower orders has permitted man to reign supreme over other animals which might easily have exterminated him. They are ferocious fighters, when aroused; and, most important of all, they will obey me. They will be a protection against both beasts and men. I'll send them away now to hunt in the vicinity; but when I call, they'll come."

"Why, he talks to them!" exclaimed Helen, as Tarzan walked over and spoke to Ungo.

"Of course he does," said d'Arnot. "Their language was the first he ever learned."

"You should have seen him fight with that great bull," said Magra. "I was almost afraid of him afterward."

That night, after they had made camp, Lavac came and sat on a log beside Helen. "There is a full moon," he said.

"Yes," she replied; "I'd noticed it. I shall never see a full moon again without hearing the throbbing of that awful drum and thinking of what Magra went through."

"It should bring happier thoughts to you," he said, "as it does to me—thoughts of love. The full moon is for love."

"It is also for lunacy," she suggested.

"I wish you could love me," he said. "Why don't you? Is it because of d'Arnot? Be careful with him. He is notorious for his conquests."

The girl was disgusted. How different this from d'Arnot's praise of his rival. "Please don't speak of it again," she said. "I don't love you, and that's that." Then she got up and walked away, joining d'Arnot near the fire. Lavac remained where he was, brooding and furious.

Lavac was not the only member of the party to whom the full moon suggested love. It found Wolff recipient, also. His colossal egotism did not permit him to doubt that eventually he would break down Magra's resistance, and that she would fall into his arms. Being an egotist, he always seized upon the wrong thing to say to her, as he did when he caught her alone that evening.

"What do you see in that damn monkey-man?" was his opening sally in the game of love. "He ain't got nothin' but a G string to his name. Look at me! I got £2000 and a half interest in the biggest diamond in the world."

"I am looking at you," replied Magra. "Perhaps that's one of the reasons I don't like you. You know, Wolff, there must be a lot of different words to describe a person like you; but I don't know any of them that are bad enough to fit you. I wouldn't have you if you owned the father and mother of diamonds, both, and were the last man on Earth into the bargain. Now, don't ever mention this subject to me again, or I'll tell the 'monkey-man' on you; and he'll probably break you in two and forget to put you back together again. You know, he isn't in love with you either."

"You think you're too good for me, do you?" growled Wolff. "Well, I'll show you. I'll get you; and I'll get your dirty monkey-man, too."

"Don't let him see you doing it," laughed Magra.

"I ain't afraid of him," boasted Wolff.

"Say, you wouldn't even dare stab Tarzan in the back. You know, I saw you running away when that ape grabbed me. No, Wolff, you don't scare me worth a cent. Everybody in this camp has your number, and I know just what sort of a yellow double-crosser you are."

13

As THE BARGE in which Thome and Taask were prisoners was being rowed up the river, the former heard one of the warriors speak to a black galley slave in Swahili.

"Why did you take us prisoners?" he asked the warrior in command, speaking in Swahili; "and what are you going to do with us?"

"I took you prisoners because you were too near The Forbidden City," replied the warrior. "No one may approach Ashair and return to the outer world. I am taking you there now. What will become of you rests in the hands of Queen Atka, but you may rest assured that you will never leave Ashair."

Just ahead of the galley, Thome saw the mighty wall of Tuen-Baka rising high into the blue African sky; and from a great, black opening in the wall the river flowed. Into this mighty natural tunnel the galley was steered. A torch was lighted and held in the bow, as the craft was rowed into the Stygian darkness ahead; but at last it emerged into the sunlight and onto the bosom of a lake that lay at the bottom of the great crater of Tuen-Baka.

Ahead and to the left, Thome saw the domes of a small, walled city. To right and left, beyond the lake, were forest and plain; and in the far distance, at the upper end of the lake, another city was dimly visible.

"Which is Ashair?" he asked a warrior.

The man jerked a thumb in the direction of the nearer city at the left. "There is Ashair," he said. "Take a good look at it, for, unless Atka sentences you to the galleys, you'll never see the outside of it again."

"And the other city?" asked Thome. "What is that?"

"That's Thobos," replied the man. "If you happen to be sentenced to a war galley, you may see more of Thobos, when we go there to fight."

As the galley approached Ashair, Atan Thome turned to Lal Taask, who sat beside him in the stern. Thome had been looking at the city, but Lal Taask had been gazing down into the clear depths of the lake.

"Look!" exclaimed Thome. "My dream come true! There is The Forbidden City; there, somewhere, lies The Father of Diamonds. I am coming closer and closer to it. It is Fate! I know now that it is written that I shall possess it."

Lal Taask shook his head. "These warriors have sharp spears," he said. "There are probably more warriors in Ashair. I do not think they will let you take The Father of Diamonds away with you. I even heard one say that we should never leave, ourselves. Do not get your hopes too high. Look down into this lake instead. The water is so clear, you can see the bottom. I have seen many fish and strange creatures such as I have never seen before. It is far more interesting than the city, and it may be the only

71

time we shall ever look at it. By the beard of the prophet, Atan Thome! Look! There is a marvel, indeed, master."

Thome looked over the side of the galley; and the sight that met his eyes wrung an exclamation of surprise and incredulity from him, for, clearly discernible at the bottom of the lake, there was a splendid temple. He could see lights shining from its windows, and as he watched it, spellbound, he saw a grotesque, man-like figure emerge from it and walk on the bottom of the lake. The creature carried a trident, but what it was doing and where it was going Atan Thome was doomed not to discover, for the rapidly propelled barge passed over the creature and the temple; and they were lost to view, as the craft approached the quay of The Forbidden City.

"Come!" commanded the warrior in charge of the party, and Thome and Taask were herded off the galley onto the quay. They entered the city through a small gateway, and were led through narrow, winding streets to a large building near the center of the city. Before the gate stood armed warriors who, after a brief parley, admitted the captives and their guard; then Atan Thome and Lal Taask were escorted into the building and into the presence of an official, who listened to the report of their captors and then spoke to them in Swahili.

The man listened to Thome's explanation of their presence near Ashair; then he shrugged. "You may be telling the truth, or you may be lying," he said. "Probably you are lying, but it makes no difference. Ashair is a forbidden city. No stranger who enters Tuen-Baka may leave alive. What becomes of him here—whether he be destroyed immediately or permitted to live for what ever useful purpose he may serve—rests wholly with the discretion of the Queen. Your capture will be reported to her; when it suits her convenience, your fate will be decided."

"If I might have audience with her," said Thome, "I am sure that I can convince her that my motives are honorable and that I can give Ashair valuable service. I have information of the greatest importance to her and to Ashair."

"You may tell me," said the official. "I will communicate the information to her."

"I must give it to the Queen in person," replied Atan Thome.

"The Queen of Ashair is not in the habit of granting audiences to prisoners," said the man, haughtily. "It will be well for you if you give this information to me—if you have any."

Atan Thome shrugged. "I have it," he said, "but I shall give it to no one but the Queen. If disaster befalls Ashair, the responsiblity will rest with you. Don't say that I didn't warn you."

"Enough of this impudence!" exclaimed the official. "Take them away and lock them up—and don't overfeed them."

"Master, you should not have antagonized him," said Lal Taask, as the two men lay on cold stone, chained to the wall of a gloomy dungeon. "If you had information to impart to the Queen—and Allah alone knows what it might be—why did you not tell the man what it was? Thus it would have reached the Queen."

"You are a good servant, Lal Taask," said Thome; "and you wield a knife with rare finesse. These are accomplishments worthy of highest encomiums, but you lack versatility. It is evident that Allah felt he had given you sufficient gifts when he gave you these powers; so he gave you nothing with which to think."

"My master is all-wise," replied Lal Taask. "I pray that he may think me out of this dungeon."

"That's what I am trying to do. Don't you realize that it would be useless to appeal to underlings? This Queen is all-powerful. If we can reach her, personally, we place our case directly before the highest tribunal; and I can plead our case much better than it could be pled second hand by one who had no interest in us."

"Again I bow to your superior wisdom," said Lal Taask, "but I am still wondering what important information you have to give the Queen of Ashair."

"Lal Taask, you are hopeless," sighed Thome. "The information I have to give to the Queen should be as obvious to you as a fly on the end of your nose."

For days, Atan Thome and Lal Taask lay on the cold stone of their dungeon floor, receiving just enough food to keep them alive; and having all Atan Thome's pleas for an audience with the Queen ignored by the silent warrior who brought their food.

"They are starving us to death," wailed Lal Taask.

"On the contrary," observed Atan Thome, "they appear to have an uncanny sense of the calorific properties of food. They know just how much will *keep* us from starving to death. And look at my waist line, Lal Taask! I have often had it in mind to embark upon a rigid diet for the purpose of reducing. The kind Asharians have anticipated that ambition. Presently, I shall be almost sylphlike."

"For you, perhaps, that may be excellent, master; but for me, who never had an ounce of surplus fat beneath his hide, it spells disaster. Already, my backbone is chafing my navel."

"Ah," exclaimed Atan Thome, as footfalls announced the approach of some one along the corridor leading to their cell, "here comes Old Garrulity again."

"I did not know that you knew his name, master," remarked Taask; "but some one accompanies him this time —I hear voices."

"Perhaps he brings an extra calorie, and needs help," suggested Thome. "If he does, it is yours. I hope it is celery."

"You like celery, master?"

"No. It shall be for you. Celery is reputed to be a brain food."

The door to the cell was unlocked, and three warriors entered. One of them removed the chains from the prisoners' ankles.

"What now?" asked Atan Thome.

"The Queen has sent for you," replied the warrior.

The two men were led through the palace to a great room, at the far end of which, upon a dais, a woman sat upon a throne hewn from a single block of lava. Warriors flanked her on either side, and slaves stood behind her throne ready to do her every bidding.

As the two men were led forward and halted before the dais, they saw a handsome woman, apparently in her early thirties. Her hair was so dressed that it stood out straight from her head in all directions to a length of eight or ten inches and had woven into it an ornate

74

headdress of white plumes. Her mien was haughty and arrogant as she eyed the prisoners coldly, and Atan Thome read cruelty in the lines of her mouth and the latent fires of a quick temper in the glint of her eyes. Here was a women to be feared, a ruthless killer, a human tigress. The equanimity of the smug Eurasian faltered before a woman for the first time.

"Why came you to Ashair?" demanded the Queen.

"By accident, majesty; we were lost. When we found our way blocked, we turned back. We were leaving the country when your warriors took us prisoner."

"You have said that you have valuable information to give me. What is it? If you have imposed upon me and wasted my time, it shall not be well for you."

"I have powerful enemies," said Atan Thome. "It was while trying to escape from them that I became lost. They are coming to Ashair to attempt to steal a great diamond which they believe you to possess. I only wished to befriend you and help you trap them."

"Are they coming in force?" asked Atka.

"That, I do not know," replied Thome; "but I presume they are. They have ample means."

Queen Atka turned to one of her nobles. "If this man has spoken the truth, he shall not fare ill at our hands. Akamen, I place the prisoners in your charge. Permit them reasonable liberties. Take them away." Then she spoke to another. "See that the approaches to Ashair are watched."

Akamen, the noble, conducted Atan Thome and Lal Taask to pleasant quarters in a far wing of the palace. "You are free to go where you will inside the palace walls, except to the royal wing. Nor may you go beneath the palace. There lie the secrets of Ashair and death for strangers."

"The Queen has been most magnanimous," said Thome. "We shall do nothing to forfeit her good will. Ashair is most interesting. I am only sorry that we may not go out into the city or upon the lake."

"It would not be safe," said Akamen. "You might be captured by a galley from Thobos. They would not treat you as well as Atka has."

"I should like to look down again at the beautiful building at the bottom of the lake," said Thome. "That was my reason for wishing to go upon the lake. What is the building? and what the strange creature I saw coming from it?"

"Curiosity is often a fatal poison," said Akamen.

14

THE TRAIL OF Atan Thome's safari was not difficult to follow, and the Gregory party made good time along it without encountering any obstacles to delay them. The general mistrust of Wolff, the doubts concerning Magra's position among them, and the moody jealousy of Lavac added to the nervous strain of their dangerous existence; and the hardships they had undergone had told upon their nerves; so that it was not always a happy company that trudged the day's trails. Only Tarzan remained serene and unruffled.

It was midday, and they had halted for a brief rest, when Tarzan suddenly became alert. "Natives are coming," he said. "There are a number of them, and they are very close. The wind just changed and brought their scent to me."

"There they are now," said Gregory. "Why, it's another safari. There are porters with packs, but I see no white men."

"It is your safari, bwana," said Ogabi. "It is the safari that was to have met you at Bonga."

"Then is must be the one that Thome stole," said d'Arnot, "but I don't see Thome."

"Another mystery of darkest Africa, perhaps," suggested Helen.

Mbuli, leading his people back toward Bonga, halted in surprise as he saw the little party of whites, then, seeing that his men greatly outnumbered them, he came forward, swaggering a little.

"Who are you?" demanded Tarzan.

"I am Mbuli," replied the chief.

"Where are your bwanas? You have deserted them."

"Who are you, white man, to question Mbuli?" demanded the native, arrogantly, the advantage of numbers giving him courage.

"I am Tarzan," replied the ape-man.

Mbuli wilted. All the arrogance went out of him. "Forgive, bwana," he begged. "I did not know you, for I have never seen you before."

"You know the law of the safari," said Tarzan. "Those who desert their white masters are punished."

"But my people would not go on," explained Mbuli. "When we came to Tuen-Baka, they would go no farther. They were afraid, for Tuen-Baka is taboo."

"You took all their equipment," continued the ape-man, glancing over the loads that the porters had thrown to the ground. "Why, you even took their food."

"Yes, bwana; but they needed no food—they were about to die—Tuen-Baka is taboo. Also, Bwana Thome lied to us. We had agreed to serve Bwana Gregory, but he told us Bwana Gregory wished us to accompany him instead."

"Nevertheless, you did wrong to abandon him. To escape punishment, you will accompany us to Tuen-Baka —we need porters and askaris."

"But my people are afraid," remonstrated Mbuli.

"Where Tarzan goes, your people may go," replied the ape-man. "I shall not lead them into danger needlessly."

"But, bwana—"

"But nothing," snapped Tarzan; then he turned to the porters. "Up packs! You are going back to Tuen-Baka."

The porters grumbled; but they picked up their packs and turned back along the trail they had just travelled, for the will of the white man was supreme; and, too, the word had spread among them that this was the fabulous Tarzan who was half man and half demon.

For three days they trekked back along the trail toward Ashair, and at noon on the seventh day the safari broke from the forest beside a quiet river. The terrain ahead was rocky and barren. Above low hills rose the truncated cone of an extinct volcano, a black, forbidding mass.

"So that is Tuen-Baka," said d'Arnot. "It is just an old volcano, after all."

"Nevertheless, the boys are afraid," said Tarzan. "We shall have to watch them at night or they'll desert again. I'm going on now to see what lies ahead."

"Be careful," cautioned d'Arnot. "The place has a bad reputation, you know."

"I am always careful," replied Tarzan.

D'Arnot grinned. "Sometimes you are about as careful of yourself as a Paris taxi driver is of pedestrians."

Tarzan followed a dim trail that roughly paralleled the river, the same trail that Lal Taask and Atan Thome had followed. As was his custom, he moved silently with every sense alert. He saw signs of strange animals and realized that he was in a country that might hold dangers beyond his experience. In a small patch of earth among the boulders and rough lava rocks, he saw the imprint of a great foot and caught faintly the odor of a reptile that had passed that way recently. He knew, from the size of the footprint, that the creature was large; and when he heard ahead of him an ominous hissing and roaring, he guessed that the maker of the footprint was not far off. Increasing his speed, but not lessening his caution, he moved forward in the direction of the sound; and coming to the edge of a gully, looked down to see a strangely garbed white warrior facing such a creature as Tarzan had never seen on earth. Perhaps he did not know it, but he was looking at a small edition of the terrible Tyrannosaurus Rex, that mighty king of carnivorous reptiles which ruled the earth eons ago. Perhaps the one below him was tiny compared with his gigantic progenitor; but he was still a formidable creature, as large as a full grown bull.

Tarzan saw in the warrior either a hostage or a means of securing information concerning this strange country and its inhabitants. If the dinosaur killed the man, he would be quite valueless; so, acting as quickly as he thought, he leaped from the cliff just as the brute charged. Only a man who did not know the meaning of fear would have taken such a risk.

The warrior facing the great reptile with his puny spear was stunned to momentary inaction when he saw an almost naked bronzed giant drop, apparently from the blue,

78

onto the back of the monster he had been facing without hope. He saw the stranger's knife striking futilely at the armored back, as the man clung with one arm about the creature's neck. He could have escaped; but he did not, and as Tarzan found a vulnerable spot in the dinosaur's throat and drove his knife home again and again, he rushed in to the ape-man's aid.

The huge reptile, seriously hurt, screamed and hissed as it threw itself about in vain effort to dislodge the man-thing from its back; but, hurt though it was, like all the reptilia it was tenacious of life and far from overcome.

As Tarzan's knife found and severed the creature's jugular vein, the warrior drove his spear through the savage heart, and with a last convulsive shudder it crashed to the ground, dead; then the two men faced one another across the great carcass.

Neither knew the temper or intentions of the other; and both were on guard as they sought to find a medium of communication more satisfactory than an improvised sign language. At last the warrior hit upon a tongue that both could speak and understand, a language he and his people had learned from the Negroes they had captured and forced into slavery—Swahili.

"I am Thetan of Thobos," he said. "I owe you my life, but why did you come to my aid? Are we to be friends or foes?"

"I am Tarzan," said the ape-man. "Let us be friends."

"Let us be friends," agreed Thetan. "Now tell me how I may repay you for what you have done for me."

"I wish to go to Ashair," said Tarzan.

The warrior shook his head. "You have asked me one thing that I cannot do for you," he said. "The Asharians are our enemies. If I took you there, we'd both be imprisoned and destroyed; but perhaps I can persuade my king to let you come to Thobos; then, when the day comes that we conquer Ashair, you may enter the city with us. But why do you wish to go to Ashair?"

"I am not alone," said Tarzan, "and in my party are the father and sister of a man we believe to be a prisoner in Ashair. It is to obtain his release that we are here."

"Perhaps my King will let you all come to Thobos," said Thetan, rather dubiously. "Such a thing would be without precedent; but because you have saved the life of his nephew and because you are enemies of Ashair, he may grant permission. At least it will do no harm to ask him."

"How may I know his answer?" asked Tarzan.

"I can bring it to you, but it will be some time before I can do so," replied Thetan. "I am down here on a mission for the King. I came by way of the only land trail out of Tuen-Baka, a trail known only to my people. I shall sleep tonight in a cave I know of, and tomorrow start back for Thobos. In three days I shall return if Herat will permit you to enter Thobos. If I do not come back, you will know that he has refused. Wait then no more than one day; then leave the country as quickly as you can. It is death for strangers to remain in the vicinity of Tuen-Baka."

"Come back to my camp," said Tarzan, "and spend the night there. We can discuss the matter with my companions."

Thetan hesitated. "They are all strangers to me," he said, "and all strangers are enemies."

"My friends will not be," the ape-man assured him. "I give you my word that they will have no desire to harm you. In the world from which they come no strangers are considered enemies until they prove themselves to be such."

"What a strange world that must be," remarked Thetan. "But I'll accept your word and go with you."

As the two men started back toward the Gregory camp, a party of warriors embarked in a galley at the quay of Ashair, dispatched by Queen Atka to intercept and harass the Gregory expedition, against which Atan Thome had warned her in order that he might win the favor of the Queen and prevent Tarzan and Gregory from reaching Ashair. The wily Eurasian had hopes of so ingratiating himself with the Queen that he might remain in Ashair until he could formulate a plan for stealing The Father of Diamonds and making his escape. So obsessed was he by his desire to possess the diamond, that he was totally unable to appreciate the futility of his scheme.

The members of the Gregory party were astonished to see Tarzan walk into camp with this strangely appareled warrior. Thetan wore the black plumes of Thobos, and upon the breast and back of his tunic there was embroidered the figure of a bull. Their friendly greetings put him at his ease, and though the Swahili of Gregory, Helen and Lavac was a little lame, they all managed fairly well in the conversation that ensued. He told them much of Tuen-Baka, of Thobos and Ashair; but when the subject of The Father of Diamonds was broached, he was evasive; and, out of courtesy, they did not press him. But his reticence only served to whet their curiosity, as they sensed the mystery that surrounded the fabulous stone.

Late that night the silence of the sleeping camp was broken by sepulchral voices keening out of the mystery of the surrounding darkness. Instantly the camp was awake and in confusion, as the terrified natives milled in panic. So terrified were they that they might have bolted for the forest had it not been that glowing death's-heads suddenly appeared floating in the air around the camp, as the voices warned, "Turn back! Turn back! Death awaits you in forbidden Ashair."

"The Asharians!" cried Thetan.

Tarzan, seeking to solve the mystery of the weird apparitions, sprang into the night in the direction of the nearest death's-head. D'Arnot sought to rally the askaris; but they were as terrified as the porters, many of whom crouched with their foreheads pressed to the ground, while others covered their ears or their eyes with trembling hands.

Into the midst of this confusion burst half a dozen Asharian warriors. The whites met them with drawn pistols. Wolff fired and missed; then the intruders were gone as suddenly as they had come. Above the turmoil of the camp rose a woman's terrified scream.

Pursuing the grinning skull into the darkness, the apeman seized a flesh and blood man, as he had expected. The fellow put up a fight; but he was no match for the steel thewed man of the jungles, who quickly disarmed him and dragged him back into camp.

"Look!" said Tarzan to the natives, pointing to the phosphorescent mask of his prisoner. "It is only a trick; you need be afraid no more. He is a man, even as you and I." Then he turned to his prisoner. "You may go," he said. "Tell your people that we do not come as enemies, and that if they will send Brian Gregory out to us, we will go away."

"I will tell them," said the warrior; but when he was safely out of the camp, he called back, "You will never see Brian Gregory, for no stranger who enters The Forbidden City ever comes out alive."

"We are well out of that," said Gregory, with a sigh. "I don't take much stock in what that fellow just said. He was just trying to frighten us. That was what the voices and the death's-heads and the raid were for, but for a while I thought that we were in for a lot of trouble."

"Who screamed?" asked Tarzan.

"It sounded like one of the girls," said Lavac, "but it may have been a porter. They were scared nearly to death."

It was then that Magra came running toward them. "Helen is gone!" she cried. "I think they got her," and at that very moment Asharian warriors were dragging Helen into a galley at the edge of the river only a short distance from the camp. During the confusion they had deliberately caused in the Gregory camp, a warrior had seized Helen; and then they had all made off for the river where the galley lay. A palm over her mouth had silenced the girl; and she was helpless against their strength, as they hurried her aboard the craft.

"Come!" cried Thetan. "Their galley must be close by in the river. We may be able to overtake them before they can put off," and, followed by the others, he ran from the camp; but when they reached the river, they saw the galley already out of their reach and moving steadily up stream beneath the steady strokes of its long oars.

"*Mon Dieu!*" exclaimed d'Arnot. "We must do something. We cannot let them take her away without doing something."

"What can we do?" asked Gregory in a broken voice.

"I am afraid you will never see her again," said Thetan. "She is beautiful; so they will probably take her to the temple of The Father of Diamonds to be hand-maiden to the priests. No alien who enters there ever comes out alive. Tomorrow, she will be as dead to the outer world as though she had never existed."

"Is there no way to overtake them?" asked Tarzan.

"Wait!" exclaimed Thetan. "There is a bare possibility. If they camp tonight this side of the tunnel that leads into Lake Horus we might be able to do so; but it is a hard trail, and only strong men could travel it."

"Will you guide me?" asked Tarzan.

"Yes," replied Thetan, "but what can we two alone expect against a galley load of Asharian warriors?"

For answer, Tarzan raised his face toward the heavens and voiced a weird cry; then he turned to d'Arnot. "Come," he said, "you will go with us."

"I'll go, too," said Lavac. "You'll need all the men you can get."

"You'll stay here," said Tarzan. "We must have protection for the camp."

Lavac grumbled; but he knew that when Tarzan gave an order it was to be obeyed; and, scowling at d'Arnot, he watched the three men disappear into the darkness.

As Thetan led them by the way he knew, his mind was occupied by thoughts of this strange, white giant who had come into his life. His great strength and his fearlessness impressed the Thobotian, but the man seemed eccentric. That strange cry he had given just as they were leaving camp! Now, what could have been his reason for that? He was still pondering this, when he heard grumblings and growlings coming out of the night behind them and growing louder. Something was following them. He glanced back and saw a blur of great black forms on the trail behind the two men who followed them.

"Something is behind you!" he warned them.

"Yes," replied Tarzan. "My apes are coming with us. I called them before we left camp."

"Your apes!" exclaimed Thetan.

"Yes; they will make good allies, and they can go where even strong men cannot. The Asharians will be surprised to see them."

"Yes," agreed Thetan, who was very much surprised himself; and his awe increased, not for the apes, but for the man who could control them.

The way grew steeper, as Thetan led them up into the hills to reach the head of the ravine where the Asharians would camp if they camped at all.

"How much farther is it?" asked Tarzan.

"We should get there just about dawn," replied Thetan.

"If they are camped there, we should take them by surprise, for they could not imagine that any one could reach them; and consequently they may not have any one on watch."

"Poor Helen!" said d'Arnot. "What will become of her if they went on to Ashair without stopping?"

"You will never see her again," replied Thetan. "For generations my people have been trying to conquer Ashair and reach the temple and The Father of Diamonds, yet we have never succeeded. How can you hope to accomplish what we have never been able to?"

"She must be there," said d'Arnot. "She must!"

"There is a possibility," explained Thetan, "but it is only a possibility."

15

WOLFF WAS GENUINELY terrified. The weird occurrences, the raid on the camp, the show of force by the Asharians had all contributed to impress him with the grave dangers and the futility of the venture. His desire to live outweighed his avarice, and The Father of Diamonds was forgotten in his anxiety to escape what he believed to be the certain fate of the party if it sought to enter The Forbidden City of Ashair.

When, at last, the camp slept, he awoke Mbuli. "Are you and your people going to stay here and be killed or forced into slavery?" he demanded.

"My people are afraid," replied the headman, "but what are we to do? We are afraid to stay here, and we are afraid to run away from the great Bwana Tarzan."

"You will never see that monkey-man again," Wolff assured the black. "He and the frog eater will be killed by the Asharians, who will then come back and either kill all of us or take us with them as slaves. How would you like to be chained to a galley all the rest of your life?"

"I would not like it, bwana," replied Mbuli.

"Then listen to me. The girl here is in danger. I got to save her; so I orders you and your boys to take us back to Bonga. How many do you think will come with you?"

"All, bwana."

"Good! Now get busy. Have 'em get their packs together, but see that they don't make no noise. When everything's ready, you take a couple of boys and get the girl. Don't let her make no noise."

* * *

After a night of sleeplessness and terrified apprehension for the future, Helen's attention was attracted by a slight noise in the forest behind the camp where her captors had halted for the night. Dawn was breaking, its ghastly light relieving the darkness that had enveloped the little ravine and revealing to the girl's astonished eyes the figures of great apes and men stealing stealthily upon the camp.

At first she was terrified by this new menace; then she recognized Tarzan and almost simultaneously saw d'Arnot behind him; and hope, that she had thought dead, welled strong within her, so that she could scarcely restrain a cry of relief as she realized that rescue was at hand; then an Asharian awoke and saw the danger. With a shout that aroused the others, he leaped to his feet; and, guessing that an attempt was being made to rescue the captive, he seized her and dragged her, struggling, toward the galley.

With a shout of encouragement to her, d'Arnot sprang forward in pursuit while two warriors engaged Tarzan, and Thetan and the apes fell upon the others. The warrior who was carrying Helen off was almost at the galley. He shouted to the slaves to make ready to put off the moment he was aboard, but d'Arnot was pressing him so closely he was compelled to turn and defend himself. D'Arnot faced him with drawn pistol as the man raised his spear. Behind d'Arnot, another warrior, who had escaped the apes, was running to the aid of his fellow.

The Frenchman could not fire at the warrior facing him without endangering Helen, and he did not know that another was approaching from behind.

What takes so long to tell occupied but a few seconds of time, for as the warrior was about to cast his spear, Helen, realizing d'Arnot's predicament, threw herself to one side, exposing her captor; and d'Arnot fired.

Tarzan, Thetan, and the apes had disposed of the remainder of the Asharians, with the exception of the one who was threatening d'Arnot from behind. The ape-man saw his friend's danger, but he was too far away to reach the warrior who was threatening him, before the man should drive his spear into d'Arnot's back. Helen realized the danger, and cried a warning to the Frenchman. D'Arnot swung about, his pistol ready; and pressed the trigger, but the hammer fell futilely upon an imperfect cap; then Tarzan launched his spear. His target was far beyond the range of any spear but that of the Lord of the Jungle. With all of his great strength, backed by the weight of his body, he cast the weapon; and, as the Asharian was lunging at d'Arnot, it passed through his body, piercing his heart. As the man fell dead at d'Arnot's feet, Helen went suddenly weak. She would have fallen had not d'Arnot taken her in his arms.

"Whew!" exclaimed Thetan. "That was a close call, but what a cast! In all my life I have never seen one that could compare with it."

"In all your life," said d'Arnot, "you have never seen such a man as Tarzan of the Apes."

Tarzan had passed them and reached the galley, where the slaves sat bewildered, not knowing what to do; then he called the apes and ordered them into the galley among the terrified slaves.

"They won't harm you," Tarzan assured them, and when Helen, d'Arnot and Thetan were aboard, he directed the slaves to row them down river to the Gregory camp.

D'Arnot sat in the stern with his arm around Helen, who evinced no inclination to resent the familiarity. On the contrary, she seemed quite content.

"I thought I had lost you, darling," he whispered.

She made no reply, other than to snuggle closer and sigh happily, which, to d'Arnot, was at least an acceptance of his love, if not an avowal of her own. He was content to leave the matter as it stood.

Gregory, Lavac, and Ogabi were standing by the river when the galley rounded a bend and came within sight.

"The Asharians are returning!" cried Gregory. "We'd better get into the forest and hide. We three haven't a chance against them."

"Wait!" said Lavac. "That boat's full of apes."

"By George! So it is," exclaimed Gregory.

"And there is Bwana Tarzan," exclaimed Ogabi.

A few moments later the boat touched shore; and as the apes poured out, Gregory took his daughter in his arms. "Thank God, you've found her," he said to Tarzan; "but now we have some bad news for you."

"What now?" demanded d'Arnot.

"Magra and Wolff deserted with all the men and equipment last night," said Gregory.

"Oh, I can't believe that Magra would have done a thing like that," exclaimed Helen.

Gregory shook his head. "Don't forget," he reminded her, "that she was in cahoots with Thome."

"Any way," said Lavac, "she's gone."

"What are we to do now?" demanded Gregory. "It looks like the end of the trail to me."

"On the way down," said Tarzan, "I questioned some of the galley slaves. They tell me that a white man is held prisoner in the temple of The Father of Diamonds at Ashair. It may be your son. I have talked with Thetan; and he believes it may be possible that the King of Thobos will receive us kindly and even help in the rescue of your son, if there is any possibility that it may be accomplished. Under the circumstances, it may be well to go to Thobos. We have a galley, and by entering the lake after dark we should be able to pass Ashair safely."

"I should like to do that," said Gregory, "but I can't ask the rest of you to risk your lives further for me. Had I had any idea that we were to encounter such dangers, I should never have started out without a strong force of white men."

"I'll go with you," said d'Arnot.

"And I," said Lavac.

"Where Bwana Tarzan goes, I go," said Ogabi.

"Then we all go," said the ape-man.

* * *

An exhausted warrior stumbled into the presence of Atka, Queen of Ashair. "We were camped for the night in the ravine below the tunnel," he reported. "We had with us a girl whom we had captured in the camp of the strangers. At dawn we were attacked by three men and a band of apes. One of the men was a Thobotian. The leader was a naked white warrior. In the beginning of the fight, I was knocked senseless. I knew nothing more until I regained consciousness and found myself alone with the dead. The galley was gone. I think they must have thought me dead."

"Which way did they go?" demanded Atka.

"That I do not know," replied the warrior, "but it is probable that they went back down stream to their camp."

The Queen turned to a noble standing near the throne. "Man six galleys," she ordered, "and bring me those people, dead or alive! They shall taste the anger of Brulor!"

16

WOLFF HAD stumbled along the back trail all night, and his disposition had not been improved by the fact that he had had to drag a resisting Magra most of the way. He had stopped now for a brief rest. The boys had dropped their packs and thrown themselves to the ground. Wolff was wiping the sweat from his forehead and glaring at the girl.

"You might as well come along peaceable," said the man. "It'll be easier for both of us. I got you, and I'm goin' to keep you. You might as well make up your mind to that."

"You're wasting your time," replied Magra. "You can lead a horse to water, you know——"

"And I can make it drink, too," growled Wolff. "Come here, you!" He seized her and drew her to him.

With her right hand, Magra attempted to push him away, while her left hand sought the pistol at his hip. "Stop!" she cried, "or, before God, I'll kill you!" but Wolff only laughed at her and drew her closer.

He died with the ugly grin upon his face, as Magra wrested his weapon from its holster and shot him through the chest. As Wolff fell, Mbuli leaped to his feet, followed by his boys. The white girl was alone now, in their power; and Mbuli knew where she would bring a good price. Also, there were two thousand English pounds on the dead man.

Magra swung around and faced Mbuli. "Pick up your loads and get going back to camp!" she ordered. Mbuli hesitated and came toward her. His attitude was insubordinate and threatening. "Do as I tell you, Mbuli," snapped the girl, "or you'll get what Wolff got."

"We are tired," said Mbuli, seeking time. "Let us rest."

"You can rest in camp. Get going!"

Urging the men on, Magra drove them back along the trail toward camp. They grumbled; but they obeyed, for they had seen her kill Wolff. She walked behind them, with Mbuli just in front of her; and she never let him forget that a pistol was aimed at the small of his back. She would have driven them faster had she known that her companions were about to abandon the camp along a route she could not follow, but she did not know.

* * *

As the others in the Gregory camp discussed their plans, Lavac stood aside moodily, eyeing d'Arnot and Helen who stood hand in hand; and as the others went to their tents to gather a few of the personal belongings the deserting porters had left behind, he accosted d'Arnot.

"You are very familiar with Ma'moiselle Helen," he said; "and I resent it, but I suppose she prefers you because you are a captain and have more money than I."

D'Arnot, ordinarily slow to anger, flushed and then

went white. "And I resent *that,* you pig!" he snapped, slapping Lavac across the face.

"You can't do that to me!" growled Lavac, whipping his gun from its holster.

Fortunately, Tarzan chanced to be passing close to Lavac. He leaped between the two men and seized the lieutenant's gun hand. "None of that!" he snapped. "We've enough troubles without fighting among ourselves. I'll keep your gun until you cool off and get a little sense. Now, into the barge, all of you. We're leaving for Thobos at once."

"We can't have any of this," said Gregory. "If Lieutenant Lavac feels as he does, I think he had better wait here for us."

"How about it, Lavac?" asked Tarzan.

"It will not occur again," said the man. "I lost my head. If Captain d'Arnot will accept my apology, I offer it."

"Certainly," said d'Arnot. "I regret the whole affair, and I am sorry that I struck you." Then the two men shook hands quite perfunctorily, and separated coldly. It was obvious that from now on nothing but bad blood would exist between them.

"What about the apes?" asked Gregory, more to bridge the awkward silence than because he was interested.

"I have told them to stay around here for a moon and hunt," replied Tarzan. "If they don't forget it, they'll stay; unless the hunting is very poor."

As Tarzan was about to board the galley, his keen ears caught the sound of approaching footsteps from the direction of the forest. "Some one is coming," he said. "We'll wait and see who it is. Be ready to push off—they may not be friends."

Presently the head of a safari came into view, debouching from the forest. "Why, those are our men!" exclaimed Helen.

"Yes," said Tarzan, "and there's Magra bringing up the rear. You were quite right about her."

"I was sure she'd never desert us like that," said Helen. "I wonder where Wolff is."

"She's got a gun on Mbuli," said d'Arnot. "There is a woman!"

Magra herded them down to the river, where she told briefly of how Wolff had persuaded Mbuli and his men to abduct her and desert, and of Wolff's death. "I found these on him," she said, "The £2000 of which he defrauded Mr. Gregory and Thome and the map he stole from Helen's room."

"We are well rid of him," said Gregory.

Tarzan ordered the natives to load all of the supplies and equipment on board the galley, and when they had done so he dismissed them.

"You may wait here for us if you wish," he said, "or you may go back to your own country. Eventually you will be punished for what you have done."

Bending to their oars, the slaves drove the galley up stream, as the members of the party momentarily relaxed from the nervous strain of the past hours. Lavac sat in the bow, looking forward, so that he would not see d'Arnot and Helen sitting close to one another. Magra sat beside Tarzan. All were quiet, grateful for the peace and restfulness of the river. For a time, at least, their way seemed assured as far as Thobos, for they would pass Ashair by night. What their reception in Thobos would be was uncertain. Even Thetan could assure them of nothing more than that he would intercede with his uncle, the King, in their behalf; but he thought that the fact that Tarzan had saved his life and that they were all enemies of the Asharians would go a long way toward insuring them a friendly attitude on the part of King Herat.

Magra sighed and turned to Tarzan. "You have all been so splendid to me," she said, "although you knew that I was an accomplice of Thome. I want you to know that I am loyal to you now."

Tarzan made no reply. His attention was centered on another matter. The galley was too heavily laden. Its gunwales were almost awash as it moved slowly up the narrow gorge.

"We'll have to put some of this stuff ashore in that ravine where we found Helen," he said. "If we ran into

91

swift water in the river or any sort of a blow on the lake, we'd founder."

"Look!" cried Lavac. "Here comes a galley."

"An Asharian!" exclaimed Thetan, "and there are others right behind it."

"Six of 'em," said Levac.

"Good Lord!" exclaimed Gregory. "We'd better turn back."

"They'd overtake us in no time," said Thetan. "We're in for it."

Tarzan smiled. "There is nothing to do, then, but fight," he said.

"We haven't a chance, have we?" asked Magra.

"It doesn't look like it," replied d'Arnot.

"If there is such a thing as a jinx," said Helen, "we certainly have one camping on our trail."

The narrow gorge echoed to the war cries of the Asharians, as their galleys bore down on their hapless victims. Gregory's party met them with gunfire and arrows, while the short Asharian spears hurtled about them. As the men had leaped to their feet to fire over the heads of the slaves, the galley tipped dangerously, shipping water and spoiling their aim. A spear struck one of the oarsmen; and as he lurched forward, dead, his oar fouled that of another slave; and a moment later the galley swung broadside across the river as the leading Asharian galley, sped down stream by forty oars, bore down upon it. There was a crash of splintering wood as the prow of the enemy rammed the Gregory galley amidships. Already listing crazily, she careened to the impact; and as the water poured over her port gunwale, she began to sink, leaving her passengers floundering in the river and her slaves screaming in their chains; then the other galleys moved in to pick up the survivors.

D'Arnot and Helen were dragged into the galley farthest up stream, which immediately set out for Ashair. The other members of the party had drifted down stream before they were finally picked up by a second galley. Tarzan had swum beside Magra, encouraging and supporting her, while Gregory, Lavac, and Ogabi remained nearby. Night was falling, and it would soon be dark in the narrow gorge. When they were in the craft, they saw that Thetan was already there, having been picked up before they were; but Helen and d'Arnot were not there; and the boat in which they were prisoners was out of sight around a bend in the river.

"Did you see anything of Helen?" asked Gregory, but no one had.

"I could almost wish that she drowned," he added. "God! Why did I ever undertake this stupid venture?"

"It would have been better had we all drowned," said Thetan. "There is no hope for those who fall into the hands of the Asharians."

"All that has happened to us so far," said Tarzan, "is that we have gotten wet. Wait until something really bad happens before you give up hope."

"But look at what lies ahead of us!" exclaimed Lavac.

"I do not know what lies ahead of us, and neither do you," the ape-man reminded him; "therefore we might as well anticipate the best as the worst."

"A most excellent philosophy," commented Gregory, "but a strain on one's credulity."

"I think it is good," said Magra.

In the leading galley, Helen and d'Arnot sat huddled together, shivering with cold.

"I wonder what became of the others," said the girl.

"I don't know, dear," replied d'Arnot; "but thank God that you and I were not separated."

"Yes," she whispered, and then, "I suppose this is the end; but we shall go together."

"Keep a stiff upper lip, darling. Don't give up hope; they haven't harmed us yet."

"Poor Dad," said Helen. "Do you suppose he and all the others drowned?"

"They may have been picked up, too," encouraged d'Arnot.

"Little good it will do any of us," continued the girl. "No wonder poor Brian never returned from Ashair. What was that?"

An eerie scream shattered the silence of the night, reverberating weirdly in the narrow gorge.

17

ATAN THOME AND Lal Taask were taking their ease on the terrace of Atka's palace, overlooking the lake. They were treated like guests, but they knew that they were prisoners. Lal Taask would have given his soul to be well out of the country; but Atan Thome still harbored dreams of The Father of Diamonds, which he pictured as a stone as large as a football. He often amused himself by trying to compute its value; then he translated it into pounds sterling and bought yachts and castles and great country estates. He gave the most marvellous dinners that Paris had ever known, and was fawned upon by the world's most beautiful women, whom he covered with furs and jewels. But the walls of Ashair still rose about him; and, towering above those, the walls of Tuen-Baka.

As they sat there, the noble Akamen joined them. "Your enemies have probably been captured by this time," he said.

"What will happen to them?" asked Lal Taask. He was thinking of what might be going to happen to him sooner or later.

"They shall know the wrath of Brulor," replied Akamen.

"Who is Brulor?" asked Thome.

"Brulor is our god, The Father of Diamonds," explained the Asharian. "His temple lies at the bottom of Lake Horus, guarded by the priests of Brulor and the waters of sacred Horus."

"But I thought that The Father of Diamonds was a diamond," exclaimed Atan Thome, terrified by the suggestion that it was a man.

"What do you know of The Father of Diamonds?" demanded Akamen.

"Nothing," said Thome, hastily. "I have just heard the term."

"Well," said Akamen, "it's something we are not supposed to discuss with barbarians; but I don't mind telling you that The Father of Diamonds is the name given both to Brulor and The Father of Diamonds that reposes in the casket on the altar before his throne in the temple."

Atan Thome breathed a sigh of relief. So there was a Father of Diamonds after all. Suddenly there came faintly to their ears a weird scream from far down the lake toward the tunnel that leads to the outside world and carries the waters of Horus down to the sea thousands of miles away.

"I wonder what that was," said Akamen. "It sounded almost human."

"Are there any apes around here?" asked Thome.

"No," replied Akamen; "why?"

"That sounded a little like an ape," said Atan Thome.

*   *   *

"It will be very dark inside there," said Tarzan, as the galley in which he and his fellow prisoners were being taken to Ashair approached the mouth of the tunnel leading to Lake Horus. He spoke in English. "Each of you pick a couple of men; and when I say 'Kreegah,' throw them overboard. If we act very quickly, taking them off their guard, we can do it; and as soon as you have two overboard, go after more. I can't tell either Thetan or Ogabi now, as the Asharians understand Swahili; but as soon as I give you the signal, I shall tell them."

"And then what?" asked Lavac.

"Why, we'll take the boat, of course," said Gregory.

"We're likely to be killed," said Lavac, "but that's all right with me."

As the galley neared the tunnel, a warrior in the bow lighted a torch, for within the tunnel there would not be even the sky to guide the helmsman. Tarzan regretted the torch, but he did not give up his plan. Perhaps it might be more difficult now, but he felt that it still had an excellent chance to succeed.

Suddenly the ape-man sprang to his feet, and as he

hurled a warrior into the water his "Kre-e-gah!" rang through the tunnel.

"Overboard with them!" he shouted, and Thetan and Ogabi grasped the intent of his plan instantly.

Chaos and confusion reigned aboard the galley, as the five desperate and determined men fell upon the Asharian warriors, throwing or pushing them overboard. The astonished Asharians were so taken by surprise that they at first fell easy victims to the plan, but later those who had escaped the first sudden rush of the prisoners, rallied and put up a defense that threatened the success of the ape-man's bold plan.

Magra, seated amidships, was in the center of the melee. Crouched between two galley slaves, she watched the savage scene with fascinated, fearless eyes. The flaring torch in the bow of the galley painted the scene in dancing high lights and deep shadows against a background of Stygian gloom, a moving picture of embattled souls upon the brink of Hell; and through it moved, with the strength, the agility, and the majesty of a great lion, the godlike figure of the Lord of the Jungle. She saw, too, the threat of defeat that she was helpless to avert; and then she heard Thetan shout, "Help us, slaves, and win your freedom!"

Almost as one man the slaves rose in their chains and lashed out at their former masters with oars or fists. Screaming, cursing men were hurled into the black waters. A warrior lunged at Tarzan's back with his sword; but Magra caught his ankle and tripped him, and he fell between two slaves, who pitched him overboard.

As the yells and screams echoed through the tunnel, Helen pressed closer to d'Arnot. "They are fighting back there," she said.

"Yes," replied the Frenchman. "The first scream was Tarzan's warning "kreegah"; so you may rest assured that they are fighting."

"At least we know that they were not all drowned," said the girl. "Perhaps Dad is still alive, but what chance have they against all those warriors?"

"There is always a chance for the side upon which Tarzan fights," replied d'Arnot. "I'd feel much better on your account if you were back there in the galley that he's in."

"If you were there, too," she said; "otherwise I'd rather be here."

He pressed her closer to him. "What an ironical fate that we could only have met and loved under circumstances such as these. For me, it is worth the price, no matter what that price may be. But for you—well, I wish you had never come to Africa."

"Is that the gallant Frenchman?" she teased.

"You know what I mean."

"Yes; but you are still glad that I came to Africa, and so am I—no matter what happens."

Back in the rearmost galley, the last of their adversaries disposed of, the little company took stock of their losses. "Where is Ogabi?" asked Tarzan.

"An Asharian dragged him overboard," said Magra, "poor fellow."

"He was well avenged," said Lavac.

"Only Helen and d'Arnot are missing now," said Gregory. "If they weren't drowned, they must be in one of the galleys ahead of us. Is there no way in which we might rescue them?"

"There are five galleys ahead of us," said Thetan. "We are only four men. We would stand no chance against five galleys of Asharian warriors. The only possible hope that we may entertain of saving them is in enlisting my King's aid, but I have already told you that the Thobotians have never been able to enter Ashair. About the best we may hope to do is to save ourselves, and that may not be so easy if any of the galleys ahead of us are lying in wait for us. We'll have to put out our torch and take a chance in the darkness."

When the galley finally reached the end of the tunnel and the lake spread before them, a seemingly vast expanse of water beneath the dim light of the stars, they saw the glimmering torches of five galleys far to their left and just beyond them the lights of Ashair. No galley had lain in wait for them, and the way to Thobos lay open to them.

It was shortly after dawn that they approached the quay at Thobos. A company of warriors stood ready to receive them, and even though Thetan stood in full view of them in the bow of the galley, their attitude was no less belligerent.

"They don't seem very friendly," remarked Magra. "Perhaps we are jumping from the frying pan into the fire."

"Who comes?" demanded one of the warriors.

"Thetan, nephew of King Herat," replied Thetan.

"We recognize Thetan, but the others are strangers," said the warrior.

"They are friends," explained Thetan.

"They are strangers, and strangers may only enter Thobos as prisoners," insisted the warrior. "If they would land without battle, let them throw down their arms."

Under these conditions, the party was allowed to land; but they were immediately surrounded by scowling warriors. "You know, Thetan," said the leader, "that it is against the law to bring strangers to Thobos; and therefore, even though you be nephew to him, I must arrest you with the others and take you all before King Herat."

18

HELEN AND D'ARNOT were imprisoned briefly in a dungeon of the palace at Ashair; then they were summoned to appear before the Queen. As they were led into the throne room, Helen exclaimed in amazement.

"Why, there are Thome and Taask!" she whispered to d'Arnot, "there, at the side of the dais."

"So that is Thome," said d'Arnot. "I'd like to get my hands on him. They don't seem to be prisoners. I wonder what it means."

"Silence!" ordered one of their guard.

As they were led to the foot of the dais, Atka eyed

them sternly. "Why came you to The Forbidden City?" she demanded.

"To find my brother, Brian Gregory," replied Helen.

"You lie!" snapped Atka. "You came to steal The Father of Diamonds."

"The girl is innocent, O Queen," said Thome. "It was the man and his companions who sought The Father of Diamonds. If you will give the girl into my keeping, I will be responsible for her."

"The girl speaks the truth," cried d'Arnot. "She came solely to find her brother, but that man lies. It was he who came to steal The Father of Diamonds. Why else should he have come? He has no brother here. There is no other reason why he should have undertaken the expensive and dangerous journey to Ashair."

"You all lie," snapped Atka. "Send the girl to the temple as handmaiden to the priests. Imprison the men."

Suddenly, before they could prevent him, d'Arnot tore away from his guards and leaped upon Atan Thome, his strong fingers closing upon the Eurasian's throat to kill him.

"If it's the last thing in life I do!" he cried, but warriors leaped in and dragged him away before he could consummate his design.

"To the cages with him!" ordered Atka. "He shall spend the rest of his life looking at The Father of Diamonds he would have profaned."

"Good-by, Helen!" he called back as warriors dragged him from the throne room.

"Good-by, Paul!" That was all; but tears welled in her eyes as they strained after the man she loved, whom she believed she was looking upon for the last time.

As warriors seized Atan Thome and Lal Taask, Akamen stepped close to the Queen and whispered a few words to her. She nodded, and ordered the warriors to release the two men.

"I give these men into the keeping of Akamen," she said. "He shall be responsible for them. Take the girl away. Let the women purify her before she is taken to the priests."

Two warriors led d'Arnot down a long ramp to a crude elevator operated by slaves at a windlass on the floor above. They entered the cage with him, and the descent began down a dark shaft.

"I hope you took a good look at the world before you were brought into the palace," remarked one of the warriors, "for it's the last you'll ever see of it."

"Why?" asked d'Arnot. "Where are you taking me?"

"To the temple of Brulor," replied the warrior. "It lies at the bottom of Lake Horus, the sacred. You will spend the rest of your life there. It may be a short life, or it may be a long one. After you've spent a few weeks in the temple, you'll pray that it will be short."

D'Arnot could not judge the depth of the long shaft down which he was being lowered to what fate he could not guess. He might have descended two hundred feet or it might have been more. Whatever it was, he was convinced that there could be neither escape nor rescue. At the foot of the shaft, the warriors turned him over to two priests, who conducted him along a corridor that extended far out beneath the lake. At the end of the corridor, he was led into a large, oblong room, at the far end of which an old man sat upon an ornate throne. Surrounding him were priests and handmaidens, and before him an altar on which rested a large, jeweled casket.

Along both sides of the room were several cages, which reminded d'Arnot of the cages in the lion house of a zoo; but here there were no lions, only a few emaciated, almost naked men with unkempt hair and beards.

The priests led d'Arnot to the foot of the throne. "Here is a would-be profaner of The Father of Diamonds that Queen Atka has sent as an offering to Brulor," said one of the priests.

"We already have too many to feed," grumbled the old man. "Zytheb, put him in a cage."

A tall priest, carrying a great ring of keys at his belt, came forward and led the way to one of the cages, which he unlocked and motioned d'Arnot to enter. As the door clanged behind him, a sudden chill ran through the Frenchman's body as though he were entering his own tomb.

A half starved, bearded man in the next cage looked at d'Arnot curiously. "Poor devil!" he said. "Did you, too, come in search of The Father of Diamonds?"

"No," said d'Arnot. "I came looking for a man."

"What man?" asked the other.

"A man named Gregory, who is supposed to be a prisoner here," replied d'Arnot.

"Most interesting," said the man. "But I cannot but wonder what interest you would have had in looking for Brian Gregory, for, you see, I am he; and I do not recall having known you."

"So you are Brian Gregory!" exclaimed d'Arnot. "I have found you at last, but much good it will do either of us. But may I introduce myself? I am Captain d'Arnot, of the French navy."

"That makes it all the more puzzling," said Gregory. "Why should the French navy be looking for me?"

"It is not," replied d'Arnot. "I just chanced to be in Loango when your father was arranging his expedition to come in search of you, and I joined it."

"Oh, so Dad was coming after me? I hope he didn't."

"He did; and your sister, also."

"Helen? She didn't come here!"

D'Arnot nodded. "I regret to say that she did."

"Where is she? Where is Dad?"

"I don't know where your father is, but your sister was taken prisoner with me. She is here in Ashair."

"God!" exclaimed Gregory. "And I brought them to this! I and that damned thing out there in the casket."

"It is The Father of Diamonds?" asked d'Arnot.

"Yes; and that is what Brulor is called, too—The Father of Diamonds. The big diamond is in the casket, and Brulor is the god who guards it; so they call him The Father of Diamonds, too."

"The old man on the throne is Brulor?" asked d'Arnot.

Brian nodded. "The old devil!"

D'Arnot's gaze wandered about the cages and the other prisoners. "Are these all men from the outside world?" he asked.

"No," replied Brian. "Some are Asharians who have aroused the wrath of Atka, some are from Thobos, and the one in the next cage is Herkuf. He was a priest; but somehow he got in dutch with the old man, and here he is."

"And there is no escape?" asked the Frenchman.

"None," said Brian.

As the two men talked, Asharian women had completed anointing the body of Helen with aromatic oils in a chamber in the palace; and were clothing her in the scant garments of a handmaiden.

"It is fortunate for you that you are beautiful," said one of the women, "for because of that you will go to the priests instead of to the warriors or the slaves. Of course you may be chosen for sacrifice; but if not, you will not go to the warriors or slaves until you are old and ugly."

The toilet completed, Helen was taken down the long shaft and along the corridor to the throne room of Brulor; and as she entered, two men saw her and their hearts went cold. One of them called her by name as she was being led past his cage. She turned in astonishment.

"Brian!" she cried. "Oh, Brian, what have they done to you?" Then she recognized the man in the next cage. "Paul! You are both here!"

"Silence, woman!" commanded one of the priests escorting her; then she was led before Brulor.

As the old man examined her, Zytheb, the priest who carried the keys at his belt, whispered in Brulor's ear.

"What is your name, girl?" demanded Brulor.

"Helen," she replied.

"From what country do you come?"

"America."

Brulor scratched his head. "There is no such country," he said. "There is a prisoner here who said he was from that country, but I knew he was lying. You must not lie. You will get along better here if you always tell the truth. Zytheb, you will take your place beside the girl. Helen," he continued, "you shall serve Zytheb, Keeper of the Keys; and see, girl, that you serve him well. Learn the holy rites of the temple and obey Zytheb." He made some mystic passes above the jeweled casket and mumbled in a strange jargon. When he ceased, he looked up at the two standing before him. "Zytheb and Helen are now man and wife!" he announced.

"What's happening?" demanded d'Arnot.

"The old devil's married Helen to that beast, Zytheb," replied Brian with an oath; "and here we are caged up

102

like wild beasts, unable to help her. You can't know what it means to me, her brother!"

"And you don't know what it means to me, Brian," said d'Arnot; "I love her."

19

THETAN, WITH TARZAN, Gregory, Magra, and Lavac, was taken before Herat as a prisoner. Surrounding the throne of the King were black plumed warriors; and at his side sat his queen, Mentheb. Herat was a large man with a black spade beard and a smooth upper lip. His face was hard, arrogant, and cruel. He scowled, as he looked at Thetan.

"You know the laws of Thobos," he said, "and yet you dared bring strangers here. Even my nephew may not thus break the laws of Thobos with impunity. What have you to say for yourself?"

"I was being attacked by one of the great reptiles of the outer slopes of Tuen-Baka," explained Thetan. "I should have been killed, had not this man, Tarzan, at the risk of his own life, killed the beast and saved mine. When I found that he and his companions were enemies of the Asharians, I tried to help them, for I owed Tarzan a great debt. I thought, my King, that you would feel even as I. They may be strangers, but they are not enemies—they are my friends, and they should be accepted as friends by my people and my king."

Herat's scowl relaxed a little, and he sat in thought for several minutes. "What you tell me," he said, "lessens your guilt; and I forgive you, but the fact remains that they are strangers and should be destroyed. However, because of the extraordinary circumstances, I shall be lenient and give them a chance to live. Their lives shall depend upon the fulfillment of three conditions; that, in the arena, one of them kills an Asharian warrior. That is the first. The second is that one of them kills a wild lion in the arena, and the third that they bring me The Father of Diamonds from the temple at Ashair."

Thetan turned to Tarzan. "I am sorry, my friend," he said, "that I have brought you all here to die. You deserve a better fate."

"We are not dead yet," said the ape-man.

"Turn the girl over to the women. They will see that no harm befalls her," said Herat. "Imprison the men until I send for one of them to meet the Asharian. Take them away."

Warriors conducted Tarzan, Gregory, and Lavac to a cell in a dungeon and chained them to a wall. The place was damp and cold, and there was not even straw for them to lie upon.

"Hospitable country," remarked Lavac.

"At least, the King has a sense of humor," said Tarzan.

"It is reflected in his benign countenance," said Gregory.

"One of us might kill the Asharian," reflected Lavac, "but scarcely a wild lion. Well, there are three of us left. I wonder which will be the next to go."

"And I wonder what will become of Magra," said Gregory.

"Old Herat couldn't keep his eyes off her," said Lavac. "I'll bet he knows where she is."

"They turned her over to the women," said Tarzan. "I hope Thetan will be able to help her."

"She's going to need help," remarked Lavac, "and there will be none."

*　　*　　*

In Ashair, Atan Thome and Lal Taask sat in a pleasant room with the noble Akamen. If the wages of sin are death, it must have been that the paymaster was napping, for Atan Thome and Lal Taask seemed launched upon a life of ease and luxury.

"It is fortunate for you," said Akamen, "that I have influence with the Queen; otherwise, you would both be languishing in the cages of the temple of Brulor; and I can assure you that that is not a pleasant place to be."

104

"We owe you a great debt of gratitude, my friend," replied Atan Thome.

"One which you will be able to repay, perhaps," said Akamen. "You will recall what I told you."

Atan Thome nodded. "Yes," he said; "that you are cousin of the Queen and that when she dies, you will be King."

"Quite right," said Akamen; "but the most important to you is that if I were King, your lives would no longer be in danger; and, if you so desired, it might be arranged that you leave Ashair and return to your own country."

"With your guidance and advice, most noble Akamen," Atan Thome assured him, "I am sure that it can be accomplished most expeditiously."

* * *

Gregory and Lavac were stiff and lame when they awoke the following morning after a night of fitful slumber. Tarzan, inured to hardships, had fared better.

"Lord, what a night!" groaned Gregory. "If the builders of this place had searched every geological formation of the earth's crust they couldn't have found any stone harder than these lava slabs."

"Nor colder," added Lavac. "Don't you suppose there is any way in which we could escape? I'd rather take any risk than stay here. Couldn't we overpower whomever brings our food?"

"Quiet!" cautioned Tarzan. "Some one is coming."

The others had heard nothing. It was the keen ears of the ape-man which had caught the faint sound of sandals on the stone floor of the corridor leading to the cell. A moment later a key was turned in the lock, and three warriors entered.

"One of you is to fight an Asharian," said one. "He is a giant, a famous killer of men. If he wins, and he will, he gets his freedom. Which one of you wishes to be killed first?"

"Let me go," said Lavac. "I would as soon be dead as here."

"No," said Gregory. "Let me go. I am old."

"I shall go," said Tarzan, "and I shall not be killed."

The warriors laughed. "Boast while you may," said one.

They led Tarzan to a small arena, a courtyard enclosed by the palace buildings that surrounded it. At one end was a gallery for spectators, and here sat King Herat and Queen Mentheb with their court. Tarzan glanced up at them, and saw that Thetan was there, too. A guard of plumed warriors stood behind the King and Queen, and at either end of the gallery a trumpeter was posted. As Tarzan stood waiting in the center of the arena, the trumpeters raised their instruments to their lips and sounded a fanfare; and through a small doorway beneath the royal box a huge man entered the arena.

"Good luck, Tarzan!" shouted Thetan.

"He'll need it," said Herat. "A thousand to one he dies."

"Taken!" said Thetan.

The Asharian approached Tarzan and commenced to circle about him, looking for an opening. "I have killed such men as Memet," he boasted. "I shall take great pleasure in killing you."

Tarzan only growled, as early training and environment had taught him to do; but that growl brought a startled look to the face of the Asharian, for it was the growl of a lion. It shook his nerves a little, and he decided to get the thing over as quickly as possible; so he charged at close quarters with the intention of crushing his adversary in his mighty embrace. Thus he had crushed Memet, caving in his chest until his splintered ribs punctured his heart; and Tarzan let him get his hold. It was the hold he wished the other to have. The Asharian applied all the pressure of his great strength, but that mighty chest did not give an inch. He was amazed. It was unbelievable. Then Tarzan, growling, sought his foe's jugular with his teeth; and the Asharian was frankly terrified. Quickly he broke away and stepped back.

"What are you?" he cried, "man or beast?"

"I am Tarzan of the Apes. I kill!" growled the ape-man.

Like a cornered rat fearing death but forced to fight for self-preservation, the Asharian charged with lowered head; and as Tarzan sought to side step, he slipped; and the other caught him full in the chest with his head, knocking him to the ground; then the Asharian turned and leaped high in air to land upon his fallen foe and crush him.

A shout arose from the royal box. "I win!" cried Herat.

"Perhaps," admitted Thetan; "but not yet—look!"

While the Asharian was in mid-air, Tarzan rolled quickly to one side; and the other landed heavily on the flagging. Both men sprang to their feet instantly; and the Asharian, whipping a dagger from his sash, sprang at the ape-man. He had broken the rules of the contest, but he was too terrified to care about that. His only thought was to kill the beast-man.

As his foe charged with raised dagger, Tarzan leaped to one side, wheeled quickly and seized him from behind; then he swung him high above his head and hurled him to the flagging. He could have killed him then, but he preferred to play with him as a cat plays with a mouse. It was the Asharian's punishment for attempting to use a dagger; and, too, it was the humor of the jungle, which is grim and terrible.

The man scrambled to his feet; and as Tarzan slunk slowly toward him he turned and fled, begging for mercy. The ape-man pursued him; and, though he could have caught him easily, he remained just a few paces behind him, voicing an occasional growl to add to the terror of his quarry.

"Did you invite us here to watch a foot race?" asked Thetan, laughing.

King Herat smiled. "Something seems to have gone wrong with the famous killer of men," he said.

Driven to desperation by terror, the Asharian turned at bay. Tarzan stopped and commenced to circle his adversary, low growls rumbling in his throat. Suddenly the terrified man raised his dagger and plunged it into his own heart.

"You lose, Herat," laughed Thetan.

"But your Tarzan didn't kill him," objected the king.

"He frightened him to death," said Thetan.

Herat laughed. "You win," he admitted. "Send for the man. I have something to say to him."

"Never have I seen such a man," said Queen Mentheb. "Such a one should not be destroyed."

Tarzan, brought to the royal box, stood before the King and Queen.

107

"You have won your freedom fairly," said Herat, "and I am going to change the conditions. You shall be free regardless of the fulfillment of the other two conditions. The others each may win his freedom in turn."

"And the girl?" asked Tarzan. "How about her?"

Herat looked a bit uncomfortable, shooting a quick glance at his Queen, as he answered. "The girl shall not be harmed," he said, "and if all the conditions are fulfilled, she shall have her liberty. You shall remain as a guest of Thetan until your companions have either succeeded or failed; then you may leave the country. Decide among yourselves tonight which of the other two is to fight the lion tomorrow."

"I shall kill the lion, myself," said Tarzan.

"But you have won your freedom!" exclaimed Queen Mentheb. "You do not have to throw away your life."

"I shall kill the lion," reiterated Tarzan.

Herat looked questioningly at the Queen. "If he wishes to be killed, he shall," he snapped.

20

THE THRONE ROOM of the temple of Brulor was vacant except for the poor prisoners in their cages. "They have all gone, and taken Helen," said d'Arnot. "What will they do with her?"

"I don't know," replied Brian, dejectedly. "One knows nothing here. One just lives and suffers. If lucky, he may be chosen for sacrifice, and die. Sometimes they choose one of us prisoners, sometimes one of the handmaidens. It is a cruel and bloody spectacle."

As he ceased speaking, a grotesque figure entered the throne room through a doorway on the opposite side. It appeared to be a man in a skin tight suit with a strange helmet covering his entire head and an odd looking contraption strapped to his back between his shoulders. He carried a trident on the end of which a large fish wriggled. Water dripped from his helmet and his suit.

"*Mon Dieu!*" exclaimed d'Arnot. "What is that?"

"It is a ptome with our dinner," replied Brian. "The ptomes are lesser priests and greater fishermen. They go out onto the bottom of Lake Horus through watertight compartments and spear the fish with which we are fed. That affair on his back furnishes oxygen that it extracts from the water, which enters it in small quantities. They say that with one of those helmets, a man could live under water almost indefinitely, as far as his air supply was concerned. You will notice the heavy metal soles of his shoes, that prevent him from turning over and floating to the surface, feet up."

"The whole thing is quite astonishing," commented d'Arnot, "and so is that fish, for that matter. I never saw one like it before."

"You will see plenty of them from now on," replied Brian, "and I hope you like raw fish. If you don't, you'd better cultivate a taste for it—it's about all you'll get to eat here; but you'll be able to watch the priests and the handmaidens dine sumptuously. They throw a banquet in here every once in a while just to add to our misery."

* * *

Zytheb led Helen to one of the upper floors of the temple where his apartments were situated. At the end of a corridor, he threw open a door. "This is your new home," he said; "is it not beautiful?"

The room was a jumble of strange appearing furniture, with odd lamps and heavy vases. A frieze of skulls and bones encircled the walls just below the ceiling. Through a window at the far end of the room, the girl could see fishes swimming in the lake. She entered, like one in a trance, and passed through the room to stand beside a table at the window. A heavy vase of strange workmanship stood on the table, and hazily she thought how interesting it might be were her mind not in such a turmoil of hopelessness and terror. Zytheb had followed her, and now he laid a hand upon her shoulder.

"You are very beautiful," he said.

She shrank away from him, backing against the table. "Don't touch me!" she whispered.

"Come!" he said. "Remember what Brulor told you. You are my wife, and you must obey me."

"I am not your wife. I shall never be. I should rather die. Keep away from me, I tell you. Keep away!"

"You shall learn to obey and be a good wife—and like it," snapped Zytheb. "Come, now, and kiss me!"

He attempted to take her in his arms; and as he did so, she seized the vase from the table and struck him heavily over the head. Without a sound, he slumped to the floor; and she knew that she had killed him. Her first reaction was solely of relief. She had no regrets, but what was she to do now? What possibility of escape was there from this frightful place beneath the waters of Horus?

For a time she stood looking down at the dead body of the man she had killed, fascinated by the very horror of it; then slowly came the realization that she must do something. At least she could gain time by hiding the body. She looked about the room for some place where she might conceal it, shuddering at the thought of the gruesome ordeal; but she steeled herself, and dragged the body to a closet across the room. The body was heavy; but terror gave her strength, and at last she succeeded in getting it into the closet. Before she closed the door, she took the keys and his dagger. If there was any avenue of escape, she might need the keys; and she was sure that she would need the dagger.

Her first thought now was to find the throne room again and see d'Arnot and her brother. If escape were possible, she could take them with her. At least she might see them once more. Creeping along deserted corridors, she found her way down the winding stairways up which Zytheb had led her, as she searched for the throne room where the cages were. In constant fear of discovery, she came at last to a door she thought she recognized. But was this the room? If it were, would she find priests or guards within? For a moment she hesitated; then she opened the door. Yes, it was the throne room; and, except for the prisoners in their cages, it was vacant. So far fortune had favored her; and she had achieved the im-

110

possible, but how much longer might she depend upon the fickle goddess? As she crossed the room to d'Arnot's cage, she saw that the prisoners were all asleep. This fact and the quietness of the temple gave her new assurance, for if escape were possible it might be best accomplished while the temple slept. That the Asharians were confident that there could be no escape was suggested by the fact that no guards watched the prisoners, an inference that was not encouraging.

Helen leaned against the bars of d'Arnot's cage and whispered his name. The few seconds it took to awaken him seemed an eternity to the frightened girl, but at last he opened his eyes.

"Helen!" he exclaimed in astonishment. "What has happened? How did you get here?"

"Quiet!" she cautioned. "Let me get you and Brian out of those cages; then we can plan." She was trying different keys in the lock of the cage door as she talked to him, and at last she found the one that fitted.

As the door swung open he sprang out and took her in his arms. "Darling!" he whispered. "You have risked your life for this; but you shouldn't have, for what good will it do? There is no escape from this place."

"Perhaps not," she agreed, "but at least we can have these few minutes together—they can never take those away from us—and as far as risking my life is concerned will make no difference. I have already forfeited it."

"What do you mean?"

"I have killed Zytheb," she replied, "and when they find his body, I imagine they'll make short work of me;" then she told him what had happened in the apartment above.

"How brave you are," he said. "You deserve life and freedom for what you have undergone."

D'Arnot took the keys from her and unlocked Brian's cage, and as the latter opened his eyes and saw Helen and d'Arnot standing outside he thought that he was dreaming. He had to come out and touch them before he could believe his eyes. Briefly they explained what had happened.

"And now that we are out, what?" demanded d'Arnot. "There can be no escape from this place."

111

"I'm not so sure of that," replied Brian. "The priests have a secret passage that can be used if the windlass fails or if the temple should be in danger of flooding."

"Little good that will do us," said d'Arnot, "unless you know where the entrance to this secret passage is."

"I don't know, but there is one here who does. One of these prisoners, the one in the cage next to mine, is a former priest. If we liberate him, he might lead us out. I know he is anxious to escape. I'll wake him."

"Let's liberate all the poor creatures," suggested Helen.

"We certainly shall," said Brian; then he awoke Herkuf, the former priest, and explained what he had in mind, while d'Arnot released the other prisoners, cautioning them to silence, as they gathered around Brian and Herkuf.

"It will mean death by torture if we are caught," explained the latter, "and a life of danger if we escape, for we shall have no place to go in Tuen-Baka and must live in caves and hide for the remainder of our lives."

"I shall have a place to go," said a Thobotian. "I can go back to Thobos, and I can show the rest of you a secret foot trail out of Tuen-Baka, that only we of Thobos know."

"Anything, even death," said Brian, "would be better than these filthy cages and the treatment we receive here."

"Well," exlaimed the man from Thobos, "why do we stand here talking? Will you lead us out, Herkuf?"

"Yes," said the former priest; "come with me."

He led them along the corridor that ran beneath the lake to the bottom of the elevator shaft. For a moment he fumbled at a great slab of lava that formed a part of one of the walls of the corridor beside the shaft. Presently it swung toward him, revealing the mouth of an opening as dark as Erebus.

"You'll have to feel your way along this corridor," he said. "There are many stairways, some of them winding; but there are no pitfalls and no side corridors. I shall go slowly."

After all were inside the mouth of the corridor, Herkuf pulled the slab back in place; then he took the lead; and the long, slow climb commenced.

"It commences to look as though the impossible were about to be achieved," said d'Arnot.

"And a few minutes ago it appeared so very impossible," replied Helen.

"And we owe it all to you, darling."

"We owe it to Zytheb," she corrected, "or to Brulor for selecting the Keeper of the Keys as my husband."

"Well, whatever it was, we sure got a break at last," said Brian, "and the Lord knows we had one coming to us."

It was still dark when the nine fugitives emerged into the open air at the end of the secret passage.

"Where are we?" asked Brian.

"We are on the hillside above Ashair," replied Herkuf, "and we shall breathe pure air and know freedom for a few hours at least."

"And which way do we go now?"

"We should head toward the upper end of the lake," said the Thobotian. "It is there that the trail begins that leads out of Tuen-Baka."

"Very well," said Herkuf, "come on! I know a canyon we can hide in if we don't want to travel by day. We can just about reach it by sunrise. As soon as they find we have escaped, they will search for us; so the farther away we can get and the more secluded the hiding place, the better off we shall be."

21

IN NO DUNGEON had Magra been incarcerated, but in well appointed apartments with slave women to attend her. She wondered why she had been accorded these luxuries, until the door opened and King Herat entered; then she guessed the reason for her preferment. He wore an ingratiating smile and the self-satisfied look of a cat that has cornered a canary.

"You are being well treated and well served?" asked Herat.

"Yes, Your Majesty," replied Magra.

"I am glad; I wish you to be happy. You are my guest, you know," he explained.

"That is very kind of you. I hope you are treating my companions as generously."

"Scarcely," he replied, "though I have been very fair and lenient with them; but do you know why I am treating you so well?"

"Because the Thobotians are a kindly people, I suppose," she replied, "and their King a kindly king."

"Bosh!" exclaimed Herat. "It is because you are beautiful, my dear; and because you please me. Those who please a king may fair very well indeed." He came toward her. "I shall see that you live like a queen," he said, suddenly taking her into his arms.

"I shall not please you for long," she snapped, "nor will you ever be pleased by anything again if you don't get out of here and leave me alone," and as she spoke, she snatched his dagger from its sheath and pressed the point of it against his side.

"You she-devil!" he cried, as he jumped away. "You'll pay for this."

"I think not," said Magra, "but you shall, if you annoy me or try to punish me."

"You dare threaten me, slave!"

"I certainly do," Magra assured him; "and it is no idle threat, either."

"Huh!" sneered Herat. "What can you do, other than threaten?"

"I can see that the Queen learns of this. My slaves have told me that she has a high temper."

"You win," said Herat, "but let us be friends."

While King Herat visited Magra, Queen Mentheb lay on a couch in one of her apartments while slave women enameled her toenails and arranged her hair.

"That story is so old it smells," said the Queen, peevishly.

"I am sorry, Majesty," said the woman who had just sought to amuse Mentheb with a story; "but have you heard the one about the farmer's wife?"

114

"About a hundred times," snapped the Queen. "Every time Herat drinks too much wine he tells it. I am the only one who doesn't have to laugh at it every time he tells it. That is one of the advantages of being a queen."

"Oh, I know one, Your Majesty," exclaimed another of the women. "It seems there were two Romans——"

"Shut up!" commanded Mentheb. "You all bore me."

"Perhaps we could send for an entertainer to amuse Your Majesty," suggested another.

Mentheb thought for a moment before she replied. "Now, there is one whom it would amuse me to talk with," she said. "That man who killed the Asharian in the arena. He is a man, indeed. Mesnek, suppose you go fetch him!"

"But, Majesty, what of the King? Other men are not supposed to come to these apartments. Suppose the King should come while he was here?"

"Herat won't come here tonight," said the Queen. "He is gaming with his nobles. He told me so, and that he would not be here tonight. Go fetch this super-man, Mesnek; and hurry."

As Tarzan and Thetan talked in Thetan's apartments, a dark-skinned slave entered. "Most noble Thetan," he said, "Her Majesty, Queen Mentheb, commands the presence of him who slew the Asharian in the arena."

"Where?" asked Thetan.

"In Her Majesty's apartments."

"Wait outside the door to guide him to Her Majesty," Thetan directed the slave; and when the fellow had gone, he turned to Tarzan. "You'll have to go," he said, "but be very careful. Get away as quickly as you can, and while you are there be as discreet as you know how to be. Mentheb fancies that she is something of a siren, and Herat is insanely jealous. I think he is more fearful of being made a fool of than anything else."

"Thanks," said Tarzan; "I shall be discreet."

As Tarzan was ushered into the presence of Mentheb, she greeted him with a winning smile. "So you are the man who killed the famous killer of men," she said. "That was very amusing. I do not know when I have seen anything so amusing or so entertaining."

"It is amusing to see men die?" asked the ape-man.

"Oh, well, he was only an Asharian," said the Queen, with a shrug. "What are you called?"

"Tarzan."

"'Tarzan'! It is a nice name; I like it. Come and sit down beside me and tell me that you will not fight the lion. I wish you to live and remain here."

"I shall fight the lion," said Tarzan.

"But the lion will kill you; and I do not wish you to die, Tarzan." Her tone was almost a caress.

"The lion will not kill me," replied the ape-man. "If I kill him, will you intercede with the King in behalf of my friends?"

"It would be useless," she said. "The law is the law, and Herat is just. They will die anyway, but you must live and remain in Thobos." Suddenly she started up. "Isis!" she cried. "Here comes the King! Hide!"

Tarzan remained standing where he was with arms folded, making no move to hide; and there the King found him when he entered the apartment.

Herat's face clouded with an angry scowl as he saw the ape-man. "What means this?" he demanded.

"I came in search of you, but found the Queen instead," replied Tarzan; "and I was just asking her to intercede in behalf of my friends."

"I think you lie," said Herat, "for, while I don't know you, I know my queen. I think I shall let you fight *two* lions."

"Her Majesty is blameless," said the ape-man. "She was very angry because I came."

"She looked more frightened at my sudden appearance than angry," observed Herat.

"You are most unfair to me, Herat," accused Mentheb. "And you are also unfair to this man, who speaks the truth."

"How am I unfair to him?" demanded the King.

"Because you have already promised that it should be one lion," she explained.

"I can change my mind," grumbled the King; "and, anyway, I do not see why you should be so concerned in the matter. You but substantiate my suspicions, and cause me to recall the young warrior whom I had to send to the arena last year. I had hoped that you would permit me to forget him."

Mentheb subsided into a pout, and Herat ordered Tarzan back to his quarters. "The lions have been starved," he said. "They will be quite hungry tomorrow."

"You should not starve your fighting lions, Herat," said Tarzan. "Starvation weakens them."

"They will still be able to give a good account of themselves," replied the King, "for starvation will make them more ravenous and ferocious. Now, go!"

It was near noon the next day that two warriors came to conduct Tarzan to the arena. Thetan had already gone to join the King and Queen in the royal box, after having assured the condemned man of his chagrin at the unfortunate outcome of the whole adventure into Thobos.

As Tarzan walked to the center of the arena and stopped, Herat turned to his Queen. "Your taste is excellent, Mentheb," he said; "the man is indeed a magnificent specimen. It is too bad that he must die."

"And I must compliment you on your good taste," replied the Queen, "for the woman also is a splendid specimen. It is too bad that she must die," and thus Herat learned that Mentheb had heard about his visit to Magra. The King looked most uncomfortable, for Mentheb had taken no pains to lower her voice; and the nobles about them overheard; so he was very glad as he saw the two lions slink into the arena.

Tarzan saw them, too. They were big lions, and he realized that his visit to Mentheb might cost him his life. One lion he might have conquered, but how could any man withstand the attack of two such mighty beasts? He realized that this was not intended to be a contest, but an execution; yet, as the lions approached, he showed no fear. One lion came directly toward him, while the other stood for a few moments looking about the arena; and when the latter started to follow his companion he was quite some distance behind him. It was this that suggested to Tarzan the only plan that he thought might prove successful against them. Had they charged simultaneously, he felt that there would have been no hope for him.

Suddenly, the leading lion made a rush and reared above the ape-man. Herat leaned forward, his lips parted, his eyes dilated. Above all things he loved a good kill; he liked to see blood spilled and bodies mauled. Mentheb stifled a scream.

Tarzan sprang to one side and leaped behind the lion; then he seized it and swung it above his head, wheeling about again as the second lion charged.

"What strength!" marvelled Thetan.

"I am almost sorry that I pitted him against two lions," exclaimed Herat. "He really deserved a better fate."

"What?" sneered Mentheb. "Three lions?"

"I don't mean that," said Herat, irritably. "I mean that such a man deserves better than death."

"Name of Isis!" exclaimed Thetan. "Look at him now!"

Tarzan had hurled the first lion into the face of the one that was charging, and both were down on the stone flagging of the arena.

"Incredible!" exclaimed Mentheb. "If he survives, the girl may live."

"And if he survives, I swear that he shall have his freedom," cried Herat, "but I'm afraid there's no hope for him. They'll both be at him in a moment."

In her excitement, Mentheb had risen and was leaning over the parapet. "Look! They are fighting one another!"

It was as Tarzan had believed that it would be. One lion, thinking that the other had attacked him, tore into his fellow; and with hideous roars and growls, the two fell upon one another, rending with powerful talons and giant fangs.

"The man has not only marvellous strength but great cunning," said Herat.

"He is superb," exclaimed the Queen.

As the two lions fought, they moved nearer and nearer to the royal box, until its occupants had to lean far over the parapet to watch them. Tarzan, too, had moved back; and was standing just below the box. In her excitement, Mentheb lost her balance and toppled over the parapet. At her frightened scream, the ape-man looked up just in time to catch her in his arms as she dropped toward him. Realizing the woman's danger in the event that one of the lions dispatched the other or the two should cease fighting and turn their savage attention upon their natural enemies, Tarzan started toward the doorway through which he had entered the arena, shouting to Herat to order it opened.

All was confusion and chaos in the royal box. Herat was shouting commands and warriors were rushing down toward the entrance to the arena, but they were to be too late. With a final shake of the dead body of his weaker antagonist, the victorious lion turned with a savage roar and charged after Tarzan and the Queen. There was no time now in which to reach the doorway; and the ape-man, lowering Mentheb to her feet, turned with drawn knife to meet the oncoming carnivore. Growling, he crouched; and Mentheb felt her flesh turn cold in horror.

"That lion will kill them both!" cried Herat—"he is a devil."

"So is the man," said Thetan.

Mentheb stood paralyzed by the bestial ferocity of the scene; and before the warriors had reached the doorway to rescue her, the lion was upon Tarzan. Eluding the flailing talons, the ape-man seized the black mane and swung to the beast's back, driving his knife into the tawny side. Roaring horribly, the lion threw itself about in an endeavor to dislodge the man-thing from its back; and the growls of the ape-man mingled with those of the carnivore, until Mentheb scarcely knew which one to fear the most.

At last the knife found the savage heart, the beast rolled over upon its side, and with a final convulsive shudder, died; then Tarzan placed a foot upon the body of his kill; and, raising his face to the sky, voiced the weird victory cry of the bull ape; and Mentheb, the Queen, stood in helpless fascination as her warrior nobles rushed to her rescue.

"He is a demon," exclaimed Herat, "—or a god!"

Mentheb commanded Tarzan to accompany her before Herat. She was still too shaken to do more than thank him feebly; and when she reached the box, she sank into a chair.

"You have saved my Queen," said the King, "and thus won your freedom doubly. You may remain in Thobos or you may go, as you wish."

"There is still another condition to be fulfilled," Tarzan reminded the King.

"What is that?" asked Herat.

"I must go to Ashair and bring you Brulor and his casket," replied Tarzan.

"You have done enough," said Herat; "let your friends do that."

"No," replied Tarzan. "I shall have to go. Neither of the others could accomplish anything. Perhaps I cannot; but I shall have a better chance, and Gregory's daughter and my best friend are there."

"Very well," assented Herat, "but we'll give you any assistance you wish. It's a task that one man cannot accomplish alone."

"Nor a hundred," said Mentheb. "We should know, who have tried it so often."

"I shall go alone," said Tarzan. "If I need help, I'll come back for it."

22

SELF-SATISFIED, CONTENTED, Atan Thome lounged at his ease in an apartment in the palace of Queen Atka at Ashair, while Lal Taask paced the floor nervously.

"I do not like it," grumbled the latter. "We shall all die for it."

"It is perfectly safe," Atan Thome assured him. "Everything is arranged, and when it is over we shall be safe, favorites of the ruler of Ashair—and that much nearer The Father of Diamonds."

"I have a presentiment," said Lal Taask, "that we shall not be safe."

"Put your trust in Akamen," urged Thome. "He will lead you to the Queen's bedroom; then you will know what to do."

"Why not you?" demanded Lal Taask. "It is you who wants The Father of Diamonds so badly, not I."

"I do not do it, because you are more experienced with a dagger," replied Thome, smiling. "Come! Have you lost your nerve?"

"I do not wish to do it," said Lal Taask, emphatically.

"You will do as I command!" snapped Thome.

Lal Taask's eyes fell before those of his master. "Just this once," he said. "Promise that you will not ask such a thing of me again."

"I promise that after tonight I shall ask nothing more of you," agreed Thome. "S-s-h! Some one is coming!"

As he ceased speaking, the door opened and Akamen entered the room. He was pale and nervous. He looked at Atan Thome questioningly. The latter nodded.

"It is all understood," he said. "Lal Taask will do his duty."

"Very well," said Akamen. "I have arranged everything. The Queen has retired. There are no guards before her door. It will be over in five minutes. Suspicion will be directed against the noble in command of the guard. The Queen disciplined him severely a short time ago, and it is known that he was very bitter. Come with me, Lal Taask."

Akamen led the way through silent corridors to the Queen's bedroom. Without noise, he opened the door; and as the assassin, dagger in hand, slunk stealthily toward his victim, Akamen, flattened against the wall of the corridor, awaited the blow that would make him King of Ashair. Seconds seemed as hours to him as he waited for Lal Taask to reach the side of the Queen's bed and strike.

He was almost there! The dagger hand was rising! And then there was sudden commotion in the room as warriors leaped from behind hangings and fell upon the would-be assassin and his accomplice; and Queen Atka sat up in bed, a bitter smile of triumph on her lips.

"Summon my nobles to the throne room," she directed, "and take these two and the man Thome there, also, that justice may be done."

When a warrior came to Atan Thome's apartments and summoned him to the throne room in the Queen's name, the Eurasian could scarcely restrain an expression of exultation, though he simulated surprise that Atka should wish to see him at so late an hour.

"Akamen," said the Queen, as the three men were lined up before the throne, "you conspired with these two strangers to assassinate me, that you might be king. One of your accomplices, hoping to curry favor with me, informed upon you. To my mind, he is even more vile than you, if that be possible; and his punishment shall be the same as yours. I sentence all three of you to the cages of the temple for life—a far greater punishment than a quick and merciful death. As added punishment, you shall all be half starved all of the time and tortured periodically, at each full moon. At the first, you shall each have one eye burned out; at the next, another; after that, you shall lose, first your right hands; then your left hands; your feet shall follow, one by one; and after that I am sure that I can devise other means whereby you may be reminded that treachery is a dangerous avocation." She turned to one of her nobles. "Take them away!"

Atan Thome, Lal Taask, and Akamen in adjoining cages were the only prisoners now in the Temple of Brulor, Father of Diamonds. Lal Taask and Akamen glared at Atan Thome, cursing him; but he seemed oblivious to everything except the casket on the altar before the throne.

"Lowest of the low!" growled Akamen. "You betrayed us. But for you, I should be King of Ashair."

"There is The Father of Diamonds!" whispered Atan Thome.

"Dog!" cried Taask. "For years I have served you faithfully, and now you have sacrificed me!"

"There lies The Father of Diamonds," droned Thome. "For that, I would betray my mother or my god."

A ptome approached, bearing a wriggling fish upon a trident. "Here is your dinner, damned ones!" he cried.

"It is not cooked!" exclaimed Atan Thome. "Take it away!"

"Sure, I'll take it away," said the ptome; "but then you'll go hungry. We do not cook the fish for such as you."

"Give me the fish!" screamed Lal Taask; "and let him starve, but not too much—he must be saved for my dagger."

"It is I who should have the right to kill him," growled Akamen—"he who kept me from being a king."

"You are both fools," cried Atan Thome. "Nothing matters but The Father of Diamonds. Help me get that, and I shall make us all rich. Think, Taask, what it would buy in the capitals of Europe! I would give my soul for it."

"You have no soul, you beast!" screamed Taask. "Only let me get my dagger into you!"

*   *   *

Tarzan and Thetan came with a warrior to the cell where Gregory and Lavac were chained. "Herat has reprieved you," explained Tarzan, while the warrior removed their chains. "You are to have freedom within the city until I return from Ashair."

"Why are you going to Ashair?" asked Gregory.

"I want to find out if your daughter and d'Arnot are there, and ascertain if there is any way in which they may be rescued, if they are there; then there is the matter of Brulor and The Father of Diamonds. To win freedom for all of us, they must be brought to Herat."

"The other conditions have been fulfilled?" asked Lavac. "You have killed the lions?"

"They are both dead," replied Tarzan.

"I shall go to Ashair with you." said Lavac.

"And I," said Gregory.

"It is better that I go alone," said Tarzan.

"But I must go," insisted Lavac. "I must do something to atone for my beastliness to d'Arnot. Please let me go with you."

"I must go, too," insisted Gregory.

"I can take one of you," replied Tarzan. "Herat insists that one of us remain here as a hostage. You may come, Lavac."

The morning was still young as Thetan bid Tarzan and Lavac farewell as they were setting out for Ashair. "I have told you all that I know of Ashair and the Temple of Brulor at the bottom of Lake Horus," said the Thobotian. "May the gods be with you!"

"I need no gods," said Tarzan.

"Tarzan is enough," added Lavac.

*   *   *

All night the nine fugitives had tramped from their last hiding place, and they were foot sore and weary. There had been no indication of pursuit, but Herkuf knew his own people well enough to know that they would not be allowed to escape so easily.

"Now that it is light," he said, "it is time that we found another hiding place."

"We are only a few hours from Thobos," said the Thobotian, "and before that I can show you the trail out of Tuen-Baka."

"Nevertheless, I think it better that we hide through the day," insisted Herkuf. "I have no wish to be caught and taken back to the cages."

"What is another day, if by hiding we can escape?" asked Brian.

"I think Herkuf is right," said d'Arnot. "We should not take a single risk, however small it may seem."

"Listen!" whispered Helen. "I hear voices. Some one is coming behind us."

"It can be no one but the Asharians who are looking for us," said Herkuf. "Quick! We'll turn off the trail here, and hide. Make no noise—just follow me. I know this place."

They moved silently along a narrow trail for a quarter of a mile, coming at last to a little clearing. "This is the place," said Herkuf. "I do not think they will look here for us. They will think that we kept on straight up the valley."

"I don't hear them any more," said Helen.

"The trouble with this," said d'Arnot, "is that now they'll be between us and where we want to go."

"I don't think so," replied Herkuf. "They won't dare go too near Thobos; so, if they don't find us, they'll have to turn around and come back. They'll pass us again later in the day, and tonight we can go on in safety."

"I hope you're right," said Brian.

Six Asharian warriors, following the trail of the fugitives, came to the place at which they had turned off. "Their tracks are plain here," said the leader. "Here's

124

where they turned off the main trail, and not so long ago. We should soon have them—remember to take the woman and the strange men alive."

Half crouching, the six crept along the trail of their quarry—a trail as plain as a board walk. They did not speak now, for they felt that the fugitives were not far ahead; but moved with the utmost quiet and stealth. Each was thinking of what Atka would do to them if they failed.

As Tarzan and Lavac followed a forest trail toward Ashair, the ape-man suddenly stopped and tested the air with his keen nostrils. "There are men ahead," he said. "You stay here; I'll take to the trees and investigate."

"They must be men from Ashair," said Lavac, and Tarzan nodded and was off into the trees.

Lavac watched him until he disappeared among the foliage, marvelling at his strength and agility. Though he had seen him take to the trees many times, it never ceased to thrill him; but when Tarzan was gone, he felt strangely alone and helpless.

As the ape-man swung through the trees, the scent spoor became plainer; and among that of many men he detected the delicate aroma of a white woman. It was faintly familiar but still too tenuous to identify—just a suggestion of familiarity, but it spurred him to greater speed; and while he swung silently through the lower terrace of the forest, the six Asharian warriors broke into the clearing upon the fugitives with shouts of triumph. Some of the nine started to run, bringing a shower of spears upon them; but d'Arnot, Helen, Brian, and Herkuf stood still, knowing that there could be no escape now. A spear drove through one of the fleeing men; and, as he fell, screaming, the others gave up hope and stopped.

Tarzan heard the shouts of the Asharians as they broke into the clearing and the scream of him who had received the spear. The sounds were close, now. In another moment he would be on the scene.

The Asharians, having recovered their spears, rounded up the fugitives and commenced to belabor them with the hafts of their weapons. They struck indiscriminately, venting their hatred on all; but when one of them threatened Helen, d'Arnot knocked him down; and instantly an-

125

other raised his spear to drive it through the Frenchman's back. It was this scene upon which Tarzan looked as he reached the edge of the clearing.

As Helen screamed in horror and warning, an arrow pierced the warrior's heart; and, shrieking, he fell dead. Instantly the other Asharians looked about, but they saw no one who could have sped the missile. They knew that it could not have come from any of the unarmed prisoners, and they were frightened and mystified. Only d'Arnot could even hazard a guess as to the identity of the bowman.

"It seems incredible," he whispered to Helen, "but who in the world but Tarzan could have shot that arrow?"

"Oh, if it only were!" she exclaimed.

None knew better than Tarzan of the Apes how to harass and mystify an enemy. He had seen the surprise that the mysterious messenger of death had caused in the clearing below. A grim half-smile touched his lips as he drew his bow again and selected another victim; then he sped the arrow.

Once again the mysterious killer had struck, and as another Asharian screamed and fell the others looked about in consternation.

"Who is it?" cried one. "I see nobody."

"Where is he?" demanded another. "Why doesn't he show himself?"

"It is the god of us outside people," said d'Arnot. "He will kill you all."

"If he doesn't kill us, Atka will," said a warrior, "if we don't bring you back to Ashair;" then the four remaining warriors sought to herd their prisoners onto the back trail toward the city.

"Let's make a break for it," suggested Brian. "They're confused and frightened."

"No," counselled d'Arnot; "they'd get some of us with their spears. We can't take the chance now."

Suddenly there burst upon the surprised ears of the Asharians a deep voice that spoke the Swahili they all understood. "I am Tarzan of the Apes," it boomed. "Go, and leave my friends!"

"We might as well die here as in Ashair," a warrior shouted back, "for the Queen will have us killed if we come back empty handed; so we are going to take our prisoners with us, or kill them here."

"Kill them now!" cried another, and turned upon Brian, who was closest to him; but as he raised his spear an arrow passed through his heart; and then, with the rapidity of machine gun fire, three more arrows brought down the remaining Asharians, while the surviving fugitives looked on in amazement.

"There is only one man in the world who could have done that," said d'Arnot, "and we are very fortunate that he is our friend."

As Tarzan dropped to the ground among them, they surrounded him, voicing their thanks; but he silenced them with a gesture. "What are your plans?" he asked.

"There is a Thobotian with us who is going to show us a secret trail out of Tuen-Baka," explained d'Arnot. "We didn't know that anyone but us was left alive."

"Have you seen anything of Dad?" interrupted Helen. "Was he drowned?"

"No," replied Tarzan; "he and Magra are in Thobos and safe for the moment. Lavac is back there on the trail waiting for me. He and I were on our way to Ashair to look for you."

"Then we can all turn back to Thobos," said Brian.

"It is not as simple as that," replied Tarzan. "I shall have to go to Ashair and bring back a god and a diamond to Herat before he will release your father and Magra."

"It looks like a mansize job," commented d'Arnot, with a rueful smile. "I shall go with you."

"And I," said Helen.

Tarzan shrugged. "You'd be little better off in Thobos," he said, "and I doubt very much that you could ever make it back to Bonga if you succeeded in getting out of Tuen-Baka alive."

"I think we should all stick together," said Brian. "I'm going along with you."

"My duty lies near Ashair," said Herkuf. "I shall go with you. Perhaps, of all of us, I can be of the most help in getting what you want."

"Very well," agreed the ape-man. "I'll go back and bring Lavac."

A half hour later the little party was on its way back to Ashair, the Forbidden City of Tuen-Baka.

23

As Magra sat in her apartment in the palace of Herat musing over the strange series of adventures that had brought her to this half civilized, half barbaric city, and dreaming of the godlike man she had come to love, the door opened; and the King entered.

Magra rose and faced him. "You should not come here," she said. "It will do you no good and only endanger my life. The Queen knew of the other time. She will know of this, and she will have me killed."

"Have no fear," said Herat, "for I am king."

"You only think you are," snapped Magra contemptuously.

"I am Herat, the King!" cried the monarch. "No one speaks to me like that, woman."

"Oh, they don't, don't they?" demanded an angry voice behind him; and, turning, he saw the Queen standing in the doorway. "So I have caught you at last!" she cried. "So no one speaks to you like that, eh? You haven't heard anything yet; wait 'til I get you alone!" She turned her blazing eyes on Magra. "And as for you, trollop; you die tomorrow!"

"But, my dear," expostulated Herat.

" 'But' me nothing!" snapped Mentheb. "Get out of here!"

"I thought that you said you were king," taunted Magra; then they were both gone, and the girl was left alone. Never in her life had she felt so much alone, so helpless and so hopeless. She threw herself upon a couch; and, had she been another woman, she would have burst into tears; but Magra had never cried for herself. Self-pity was not for her. She had said once that it was like cheating at solitaire, for nobody else knew about it and nobody cared and no one was hurt but herself. How she wished that Tarzan were here! He would have helped her—not with useless commiseration; but with action. He would have found a way to save her. She wondered if he would grieve for her; and then she smiled, for she knew that the philosophy of the wild beast had little place for grief. It was too accustomed to death, held life in such low esteem. But she must do something. She struck a gong that summoned a slave girl.

"Do you know where the prisoners, Gregory and Lavac, are quartered?" she asked.

"Yes, my mistress."

"Take me to them!"

When she entered Gregory's apartment, she found Thetan with him. At first she hesitated to talk before the Thobotian, but she recalled that he had befriended them; so she told them all that had just happened.

"I must escape tonight," she said. "Will you help me?"

"Mentheb is rather a decent sort," said Thetan. "She may come to realize that the fault is not yours, and of course she knows that it is not, and alter her decision to have you killed; but it would be dangerous to depend on that. I know you are guiltless, and I know that you are a friend of Turzan; so I am going to help you to escape."

"Will you help me to go with her?" asked Gregory.

"Yes," said Thetan. "I got you into this, and I should get you out of it. I shall help you because you are Tarzan's friends, and Tarzan saved my life. But never return to Thobos, for if you escape her now, Mentheb will never forget. Follow the trail on the west side of the lake south; it will bring you to Ashair and probably to death there—it is the law of Tuen-Baka."

A half hour later Thetan led Magra and Gregory to a small gate in the city wall and wished them luck as they went out into the night and set their faces toard The Forbidden City.

*　　*　　*

"Well," said d'Arnot, "here we are right back where

129

we started from," as the party of six reached the entrance to the secret passage to the Temple of Brulor on the rocky hillside above Ashair.

"I spent two years trying to get out of that hole," said Brian, "and now here I am trying to get back in again. That Herat certainly gave you a tough job, Tarzan."

"It was merely the old boy's way of condemning us a to death," said Lavac, "—an example of Thobotian humor. At least it was at first; but after Tarzan disposed of the bad man from Ashair and the two lions, I really believe that Herat came to the conclusion that he might acually bring back Brulor and The Father of Diamonds."

"Why does he want them so badly?" asked Helen.

"The Father of Diamonds belongs in Thobos," explained Herkuf, "where the temple of the true god, Chon is located. It was stolen by Atka's warriors years ago when they attacked and sank Chon's galley in which it was being carried during a solemn religious rite. Brulor is false god. Herat wishes to destroy him."

"Do you think that there is any possibility that we may be able to recover The Father of Diamonds and kidnap Brulor?" asked d'Arnot.

"Yes," replied Herkuf, "I do. We have the temple key that Helen took from Zytheb; and I know where Brulor sleeps and the hours of the day that are supposedly set apart for meditation; but which, in reality, Brulor devotes to sleeping off the effects of the strong drink to which he is addicted. During these periods the throne room is deserted, and all the inmates of the temple are compelled to remain in their own quarters. We can go directly to the throne room and get the casket, and then to Brulor's room. If we threaten him with death, he will come with us without making any outcry."

"It all sounds very easy," said Brian, "—almost too easy."

"I shall keep my fingers crossed all the time," said Helen.

"When can we make the attempt?" asked d'Arnot.

Herkuf looked up at the sun. "Now," he said, "would be a good time."

"Well, how about getting started, Tarzan?" asked Brian.

"Herkuf and I shall go in," said the ape-man. "The

rest of you hide near here and wait for us. If we are not out within an hour, you will know that we have failed; then you must try to save yourselves. Find the trail over the rim. It lies somewhere near Thobos. Get out of Tuen-Baka. It will be useless for you to try to do anything for Herkuf or me or to rescue Magra and Gregory."

"Am I not to go in with you, Tarzan?" asked d'Arnot.

"No. Too many of us might result in confusion and discovery; and, anyway, your place is with Helen. Come, Herkuf, let's get started."

As the two entered the secret passage, a sentinel priest who had been crouching behind a boulder watching the party, turned and ran as fast as he could toward the nearest city gate; while, miles away, the objects of all this now useless risk and sacrifice trudged doggedly along the trail to Ashair in an effort to avert it.

Ignorant of anything that has transpired in Ashair, not knowing that his son and daughter lived and were free, Gregory accompanied Magra rather hopelessly, his only inspiration loyalty to Tarzan and Lavac, whom he knew to be risking their lives in an effort to save his and Magra's. Magra was inspired by this same loyalty and by love —a love that had done much to change and ennoble her.

"It all seems so utterly hopeless," said Gregory. "Only four of us left, pitting our puny efforts against two cities filled with enemies. If one of them doesn't get us, the other will."

"I suppose you are right," agreed Magra. "Even the forces of nature are against us. Look up at that towering escarpment of lava, always frowning down upon us, threatening, challenging; and yet how different it would all seem if Tarzan were with us."

"Yes, I know," said Gregory. "He inspires confidence. Even the walls of Tuen-Baka would seem less unsurmountable if he were here. I think he has spoiled us all. We have come to depend upon him to such an extent that we are really quite helpless without him."

"And he is going to almost certain death for us," said Magra. "Thetan told me that it would be impossible for him to escape alive from Ashair, if he succeeded in getting in; and, knowing Tarzan, we know that he will get in. Oh, if we could only reach him before he does!"

"Look!" exclaimed Gregory. "Here come some men!"

"They have seen us," said Magra. "We can't escape them."

"They look very old and weak," said Gregory.

"But they carry spears."

The three surviving fugitives from the cages of the Temple of Brulor who had chosen to go on in search of freedom rather than return to Ashair with Tarzan's party halted in the trail.

"Who are you?" they demanded.

"Strangers looking for a way out of Tuen-Baka," replied Gregory.

The three whispered among themselves for a moment; then one of them said, "We, too, are looking for a way out of Tuen-Baka. Perhaps we should go together, for in numbers there is strength."

"We can't go until we find our friends," replied Magra. "They were on their way to Ashair."

"Perhaps we saw them. Was one of them called Tarzan?"

"Yes. Have you seen him?" demanded Gregory.

"We saw him yesterday. He and his friends went back to Ashair."

"His friends? There was but one with him," said Magra.

"There were five with him. Four men and a girl went back to Ashair with him."

"Whom could they have been, do you suppose?" Gregory asked Magra.

"Do you know who they were?" she inquired of the fugitive who had been acting as spokesman.

"Yes. One was called Herkuf, and one Lavac, and there was d'Arnot, and Brian Gregory was with him and a girl called Helen."

Gregory turned very pale. Magra caught his arm, for she thought he was going to fall. "I'm stunned," he said "I can't believe that they're all alive. It's just like having people come back from the grave—I was so sure that they were dead. Think of it, Magra! My son and my daughter both alive—and on their way back to that terrible city. We must hurry on. Maybe we can overtake them. Tell us," he said to the fugitive, "where we may find them if they have not already been captured by the Asharians."

The man gave them explicit directions for locating the hidden entrance to the secret passage to the temple. "That is where you will find them," he said, "if they have not already entered the city; but do not enter. As you value your lives, do not enter the passage. If they have done so, they are lost. You might as well give them up, for you will never see them again."

"They weren't very encouraging," said Magra, as she and Gregory continued on their way; "but perhaps they overestimate the dangers—let's hope so."

Gregory shook his head. "I'm afraid they didn't," he said. "I doubt if the dangers that lurk in The Forbidden City of Ashair can be overestimated."

"It is a strange place, this Tuen-Baka," said Magra. "No wonder that it is taboo."

24

TARZAN AND HERKUF followed the dark passageway and the winding stairs down to the lava slab that closed the secret doorway leading to the corridor they must follow beneath the lake to reach the temple.

"Here we are," said Herkuf. "If the gods are with us, we shall soon be in Brulor's room behind the throne. I'll attend to him, you get the casket. I have waited years for such an opportunity to avenge Chon, the true god, and make Brulor pay for the indignities and torture he imposed upon me. I see now how I have lived through all that I have lived through. It was for this hour. If we fail, it will mean death; but if we fail I shall welcome death."

Beyond the lava slab a group of Asharian warriors, their short spears ready, awaited them, for the sentinel priest had done his duty well.

"They must be close," said the leader of the warriors. "Be ready! but do not forget that it is the Queen's command that we take them alive for torture before death."

"I should hate to be Herkuf when Brulor gets him back in his cage," said a warrior.

"And that wild man," said another. "It was he who killed so many of our warriors that night in the tunnel. I should hate to be the wild man when Atka gets him."

The lava slab was thick, and it was skillfully fitted in the aperture; so the voices of the whispering warriors did not reach the ears of the two upon the other side of it. Ignorant of the trap into which they were walking, they paused for a moment while Herkuf groped for the knob which would open the door.

And while they paused upon the brink of disaster, another detail of warriors crept up upon the unsuspecting four who were waiting at the entrance to the secret passageway, ignorant of the imminent peril that hovered just above them among the boulders of the hillside.

"At last, darling," said d'Arnot, "I can see a ray of hope. Herkuf knows the customs of the temple, and before the inmates leave their apartments again he and Tarzan will be back with Brulor and the accursed Father of Diamonds."

"I have grown to hate the very name of the thing," said the girl. "There surely must be a curse upon it and everything connected with it. I feel that so strongly that I can't believe it possible that it is going to be the means of releasing Dad and Magra. Something will happen to turn success into failure."

"I don't wonder you're pessimistic and skeptical, but this time I'm sure you're wrong."

"I certainly hope so. I don't know when I've ever so wanted to be wrong."

Lavac and Brian were sitting on the ground a few paces from Helen and d'Arnot, the former with his back toward them that he might not see the little intimacies that still hurt him so sorely notwithstanding his honest intention to give up all hope of winning the girl. He was facing up the slope of the rocky hillside above which towered the stupendous rampart of Tuen-Baka, and so it was he who first saw the Asharian warriors as they broke cover and started down toward their quarry. As he leaped to his feet with a cry of warning, the others turned; and in the instant their hopes came tumbling about their heads like a house of match wood. The Asharians were yelling triumphantly now, as they charged down the hill, brandishing their short spears. The three men might have put up a battle even against these terrific odds, futile as it would have been, had they not feared for the safety of the girl should they invite the Asharians to hurl their spears; so they stood in silence while the warriors surrounded them, and a moment later they were being herded down toward the nearest city gate.

"You were right, after all," said d'Arnot.

"Yes," she replied, dejectedly; "the curse of the diamond is still on us. Oh, Paul, I'd rather die than go back to that awful place! This time there will be no hope for us, and what I dread most is that they will *not* kill me."

As the four prisoners were being marched down to the city, Herkuf pulled the lava slab toward him; and the two men stepped into the trap that had been laid for them. They hadn't a chance, not even the mighty ape-man, for the Asharians had planned well. As they stepped from the mouth of the passageway, two warriors, crouching low, seized them around their ankles and tripped them; and, as they fell, a dozen others swarmed upon them, slipping nooses about their ankles and wrists.

"You knew we were coming?" Herkuf asked one of the warriors, as they were being led along the corridor toward the temple.

"Certainly," replied the man. "A sentry has been watching above the city, for Atka thought that you might come back to Ashair to steal a galley. It was the only way that the strangers could escape from Tuen-Baka. It would have been better had you stayed in your cage, Herkuf, for now Brulor will have you tortured; and you know what that means."

The throne room of the temple was silent and vacant, except for the three prisoners in the cages, as Tarzan and Herkuf were led in, for it was still the period of meditation, during which the inmates of the temple were compelled to remain in their quarters; and so there was a delay while a warrior sought permission from Brulor to summon the Keeper of the Keys that the cages might be unlocked to receive the new prisoners.

Presently, Herkuf touched Tarzan on the arm. "Look!" he said. "The others have been taken, also."

Tarzan turned to see Helen, d'Arnot, Brian, and Lavac being herded into the chamber; and greeted them with one of his rare smiles. Even in the face of death he could see the humor of the situation, that they who had come so confidently to conquer should have been so ignominiously conquered themselves without the striking of a blow. D'Arnot saw the smile and returned it.

"We meet again, *mon ami*," he said; "but not where we expected to meet."

"And for the last time," added Lavac. "There will be no more meetings after this one for any of us, at least not in this life. As for me, I shall be glad. I have nothing to live for." He did not look at Helen, but they all knew what he meant.

"And you all die because of me," said Brian, "because of my stupid avarice; and I shall die without being able to atone."

"Let's not talk abut it," urged Helen. "It's bad enough as it is without constantly reminding ourselves of it."

"When one is about to die by slow torture, one does not have to be reminded of it," said Herkuf. "It occupies one's mind to the exclusion of all else. Sometimes it is a relief to talk of it."

Atan Thome looked out between the bars of his cage at the six prisoners. "So we are reunited at last!" he cackled, "we who sought The Father of Diamonds. There it is, in that casket there; but do not touch it—it is mine. It is for me alone;" then he broke into loud, maniacal laughter.

"Silence! you crazy pig," growled Lal Taask.

It was then that the Keeper of the Keys came and opened the cages. "Into their dens with them," snapped an officer, "all but this fellow here." He nodded at Tarzan. "The Queen wants to see him."

Atka sat upon her lava throne surrounded by her white plumed nobles, as the Lord of the Jungle, his hands still bound behind him, was brought before her. For a long time she sat studying him with half-closed, appraising eyes; and with neither deference nor boldness

Tarzan returned her scrutiny, much as a captive lion might regard a spectator outside his cage.

"So you are the man who killed so many of my warriors," she said at last, "and captured one of my galleys."

Tarzan stood silent before her. Finally she tapped her toe upon the floor of the dais. "Why do you not reply?" she demanded.

"You asked me nothing," he said. "You simply told me something I already knew."

"When Atka speaks, the person who is thus honored makes some reply."

Tarzan shrugged. "I do not like useless talk," he said; "but if you like to hear it, I admit that I killed some of your warriors. I should have killed more that night on the river had there been more in the galley. Yesterday, I killed six in the forest."

"So that is why they did not return!" exclaimed Atka.

"I think that must be the reason," Tarzan admitted.

"Why did you come to Ashair?" the Queen demanded.

"To free my friends who were prisoners here."

"Why are you my enemy?" asked Atka.

"I am not your enemy. I wish only the freedom of my friends," the ape-man assured her.

"And The Father of Diamonds," added Atka.

"I care nothing for that," replied Tarzan.

"But you are an accomplice of Atan Thome," she accused, "and he came to steal The Father of Diamonds."

"He is my enemy," said Tarzan.

She looked at him again for some time in silence, apparently playing with a new idea. At last she spoke.

"I think," she said, "that you are not the type that lies. I believe what you have told me, and so I would befriend you. They have told me how you fought with your ape allies at the camp below the tunnel and also of the fight in the galley, for all of the warriors did not drown: two of them swam out of the tunnel to safety. Such a man as you would be valuable to me, if loyal. Swear loyalty to me, and you shall be free."

"And my friends?" asked Tarzan. "They will be freed too?"

"Of course not. They are no good to me. Why should I free them? The man, Brian Gregory, came here solely for the purpose of stealing The Father of Diamonds. I think the others came to help him. No, they shall die in good time."

"I told you that I came here to free them," said Tarzan. "The granting of their freedom is the only condition under which I will remain."

"Slaves do not impose conditions upon Atka," snapped the Queen, imperiously. She turned to a noble. "Take him away!"

They returned Tarzan to the throne room of the temple then, but they did not free his hands until they had him locked safely in a cage. It was evident that the fighting men of Ashair held him in deep respect.

"What luck?" asked d'Arnot.

"I am here in a cage," replied Tarzan. "That is answer enough. The Queen wishes us all dead."

"I imagine her wish will come true," said d'Arnot ruefully.

"Queens have but to wish."

It was a dejected and disheartened company that awaited the next eventuality of their disastrous adventure. There were only two of them who appeared to be not entirely without hope—the ape-man, whose countenance seldom revealed his inward feelings, and Atan Thome, who continually cackled and prated of The Father of Diamonds.

When life began to stir in the throne room with the ending of the period of meditation, priests and handmaidens appeared; and finally Brulor entered and took his place upon the throne, while all knelt and beat their heads upon the floor. After a brief religious ceremony, some of the handmaidens commenced to dance before Brulor, a suggestive, lascivious dance in which some of the priests soon joined, in the midst of which a plumed warrior entered from the long corridor and announced the coming of the Queen. Instantly the music and the dancing stopped, and the dancers took their places in sanctimonious attitudes about the throne of Brulor. A loud fanfare of trumpets billowed from the mouth of the corridor, and a moment later the head of a procession appeared and marched down the center of the room toward the dais where Brulor sat. Surrounded by warriors, the Queen moved majestically to the dais, where she took her place in a second throne chair that stood beside Brulor's.

A long and tedious ceremony ensued, after which the Queen pronounced sentence upon the new prisoners, a privilege she occasionally usurped to the chagrin of Brulor, who was a god only on sufferance of the Queen.

"Let all but the woman," ordered Atka, "be offered in sacrifice, each in his turn, and with slow torture, that their spirits may go out into the world of barbarians to warn others never to seek entry to The Forbidden City of Ashair."

She spoke in a loud voice that could be heard throughout the chamber; and her words brought a ray of hope to d'Arnot, for Helen had not been sentenced to torture and death, but his hopes were dashed by the Queen's next words.

"The woman shall be taken to the little chamber to die slowly as a sacrifice to Holy Horus. This shall be her punishment for the killing of Zytheb, the priest. Let her be taken away at once. The sentences of the others shall be carried out at the discretion of Brulor."

A priest scurried from the throne room to return presently with three ptomes, one of which carried an extra water suit and helmet. The Keeper of the Keys led them to Helen's cage, which he unlocked, after which the ptomes entered, removed the girl's outer clothing and dressed her in the water suit. Before they placed the helmet over her head she turned toward d'Arnot, who stood with ashen face pressed against the partition bars that separated their cages.

"Once more, good-by," she said. "It will not be for long now."

Emotion stifled the man's reply; and tears blinded him, as the ptomes fitted the helmet over Helen's head; then they led her away. He watched until she passed from sight through a doorway on the opposite side of the temple; then he sank to the floor of his cage and buried his head in his arms. Brian Gregory cursed aloud. He cursed Atka and Brulor and The Father of Diamonds, but most of all he cursed himself.

The Queen and her entourage left the temple, and presently Brulor and the priests and the handmaidens were gone, leaving the doomed men to their own unhappy company. Atan Thome jabbered incessantly about The Father of Diamonds, while Lal Taask and Akamen threatened and reviled him. Lavac sat on his haunches staring at the doorway through which Helen had disappeared to pass out of his life forever, but he knew that she was no more lost to him than she had been before. Brian paced the length of his cage, mumbling to himself. Tarzan and Herkuf spoke together in low tones. D'Arnot was almost ill from desperation and hopelessness. He heard Tarzan asking many questions of Herkuf, but they made no impression on him. Helen was gone now forever. What difference did anything else make? Why did Tarzan ask so many questions? It was not like him; and anyway he, too, would soon be dead.

* * *

Silhouetted against the blue African sky, Ungo and his fellow apes stood at the rim of the crater of Tuen-Baka and looked down into the valley. They saw the green of the plains and the forests; and they looked good to them after the barren outer slopes of the mountain.

"We go down," grunted Ungo.

"Perhaps Tarzan there," suggested another.

"Food there," said Ungo. "Tarzan not there, we go back old hunting grounds. This bad country for mangani."

25

HELEN GREGORY was, despite her flair for adventure and her not inconsiderable fortitude, essentially feminine. She was the type that stirred the deepest protective instincts of men; and, perhaps because of that very characteristic, she subconsciously craved protection, though she would have been the last to realize it. Fortified by the knowledge that masculine aid was within call, she might have dared anything; while the realization that she was alone among enemies, hopelessly cut off from all natural protectors, left her a frightened little girl upon the verge of panic. That she did not break under the strain speaks well for her strength of character.

Her steps did not falter as the three ptomes led her from the throne room and down a short corridor, through a room where many ptomes were gathered lying upon narrow cots or playing at games, their water suits and helmets hung upon pegs against the wall, their tridents standing in racks, and along another corridor to a massive door secured by huge bolts and flanked by valve handwheels and levers. Here one of the ptomes turned wheels and pulled on levers, and they all waited while he watched a gauge beside the door.

This, she thought, must be the door to the torture chamber; and she wondered what lay behind and how long death would be in coming to her rescue. Death! Man's last refuge when hope is gone, his last friend, his life's ultimate goal. She thought of her father and of Brian and of Paul d'Arnot. They would be following her soon. She wished that she and d'Arnot might have gone together. It would have been easier for both had it been that way.

At last the door swung open and the ptomes pushed her into a cylindrical chamber, following her in and closing and bolting the door. Here were other handwheels and levers and gauges; and there was an identical door on the opposite side of the chamber flanked by similar gadgets. She saw no signs of instruments of torture, and she wondered how they were going to kill her and why they had brought her here to do it and why they all wore the strange helmets. She watched while a ptome turned a handwheel, and caught her breath as she saw water rushing into the chamber. They couldn't be going to drown her, for if she drowned, they would drown too. The chamber filled rapidly; and when it was full, one of them manipulated the wheels and levers beside the second door; and when it swung open, they led her out into the diffused light of the lake bottom.

Under other circumstances she would have been entranced by the beauty of the scene upon which the sun filtered down through the clear waters of Horus. She found

141

herself being led along a gravel path between neat gardens of marine plants which other ptomes were tending to serve as delicacies for the courts of Atka and Brulor. Strange and beautiful fishes swam about them; and great turtles paddled clumsily away as they approached, while crabs of many colors scurried from their path. Here and there were marine trees towering high, their foliage undulating gracefully to the movement of the water, while bright colored fishes played among it like gay birds among the branches of terrestrial trees. All was beauty and movement and—silence. To the girl, the silence spoke more loudly than the beauty or the movement—it bespoke the silence of the tomb.

Inside the temple she had found walking arduous and slow, impeded by the heavy metal soles of the shoes they had put on her; but here she moved as though walking on air, lightly as a feather, effortless as the passing of a shadow. She felt that she might leap high above the trees if one of the ptomes were not holding her by the arm; but these were only flashes of thought breaking occasionally the dense gloom of the horror that engulfed her.

Presently she saw ahead of them a small circular building topped by a single dome, and realized that it was toward this the ptomes were leading her. When they reached the building, which seemed to have neither doors nor windows, two ptomes seized Helen's arms, one on either side, and leaped lightly upward, carrying her with them, the third ptome following. A few swimming strokes carried them to the top of the dome, where the girl saw a circular door, which she recognized now, from the gadgets flanking it, as the entrance to an air chamber such as that through which she had passed from the temple to the lake bottom.

The chamber below was filled with water when they entered it, and it was several minutes before it emptied; then the ptomes removed her helmet and suit, lifted a trap door in the floor, pointed to a ladder, and motioned her to descend. As in the upper chamber, there was a window in the wall on the side opposite to that from which they had approached the dome, which she had previously thought windowless; and through this window the diffused light of the lake bottom dimly illuminated the interior of the circular room in which she was imprisoned. It was entirely bare—the walls, the window, and the ladder constituted her world. The ptomes had closed the trap door above her, and presently she heard water gushing into the chamber above; then it commenced to trickle down one wall of her prison, and presently the trickle became a little stream. As water covered the floor of her cell, she understood the nature of the torture and death that confronted her. The chamber would fill slowly. She might prolong life and agony by climbing the ladder, but the end was inevitably the same.

She realized what exquisite mental torture the minds of these people had conceived, that one should be condemned to die alone, drowned like a rat in a trap. She wondered if she would have the courage to end it quickly when the water was deep enough, or if she would drag out the torture to the topmost rung of the ladder.

And as the water rose slowly in Helen's death cell, Herkuf whispered to Tarzan through the bars of his cage, "It will soon be time. Do you think you can do it?"

"I can do my part," the ape-man assured him. "When the time comes, let me know."

When night came and darkness settled above Horus a faint light still filtered down through the waters to the death cell where Helen waited for the end. It was the light of heavenly stars, but it brought no hope of the doomed girl. The water was at her knees now; and she stood with one hand on the ladder, still wondering what she should do. She turned wearily; and, with both arms resting on a rung of the ladder, buried her face in them. She thought of d'Arnot and the happiness that might have been theirs had they met under different circumstances; and, even with hope gone, that thought made her want to cling to life as long as she could, for at least there was a certain sad happiness in envisioning the happiness she had been denied. She thought of Brian; and, without bitterness toward him, she execrated the avarice that had lured him to this awful place and cost the lives of so many people, people who loved him. And she prayed.

Again Herkuf whispered to Tarzan. "It is time," he said. "They will all be asleep. But the bars are very strong."

"Not so strong as Tarzan," replied the ape-man. "I have tried them—watch!"

As he spoke, he seized two bars. The muscles stood out upon his shoulders as he exerted his strength upon the insensate metal. Herkuf watched, breathless, and filled with doubt; then he saw the bars spreading apart, and a moment later saw Tarzan squeeze between them and push them back into place. Similarly the ape-man liberated Herkuf.

"You are as strong as a bull elephant," gasped the priest.

"Come!" said Tarzan. "We have no time to waste. Lead the way."

"No," replied Herkuf, "we have no time to waste. Even if we get through without delay, we may still be too late."

Silently, stealthily, Herkuf and Tarzan crossed the temple toward a closed door. The other prisoners slept. No one had seen Tarzan escape and release Herkuf. Even the bars, bent back almost to normal position, gave little evidence of the manner of their liberation; and few would have believed the truth, for many have been the prisoners who had sought to bend them; but never before had it been done.

Herkuf led Tarzan down a short corridor to the room of the ptomes; and as the priest opened the door, Tarzan saw the lesser priests sleeping on their hard benches. He saw their water suits hanging on their pegs and their tridents in the racks. The ptomes slept thus without sentries and the temple went unguarded because it was considered impregnable.

Cautiously the two men took three water suits and helmets from their pegs, gathered up three tridents, and crossed the room to the doorway on the opposite side without awakening a ptome. Once past the door, each donned a suit.

"The gods have been with us so far," whispered Herkuf, "and if we can pass through the air chamber without being discovered, we stand a good chance to succeed—if we are in time."

As the water rose to Helen's shoulders she finally gave up all thought of suicide. She would cling to life to the last moment. They might rob her of that; but they could

144

not rob her of her courage, and as the water rose still higher she stepped to the lowest rung of the ladder.

Reminiscences rioted through her mind as she waited for death, and pleasant thoughts and bitter. She pondered the futility of man's quest for sudden wealth and of the evil and suffering it entailed. Of what avail would success be now to either Brian or Thome if, by some chance, it should come to one of them? for one had lost his sister and, perhaps, his father; and the other had lost his mind. Now the water forced her up to a higher rung of the ladder. Step by step, she was climbing to her rendezvous with Death.

Herkuf and Tarzan passed safely through the air chamber out into the water of the lake. Through the garden of the ptomes they made their way toward the watery cell where Death was creeping relentlessly upon Helen Gregory, and dark shapes glided sinuously about them in this mysterious world of silence.

At last they reached the air chamber above Helen's cell; and Herkuf started the pump that would eject the water, but it seemed to both men that it would never empty the chamber. They knew that the water had been rising for hours in the death cell beneath them and that death might come to the girl before they reached her, if she were not already dead.

Just below them, clinging to the last few precious moments of life, Helen had ascended the ladder as far as she could go; but the water pursued her relentlessly. Already her head was touching the ceiling. She could climb no farther. The cold hand of Death caressed her cheek. Suddenly she became alert, listening. She heard noises in the chamber above. What might they signify? Not rescue, certainly; perhaps some new torture.

At last the air chamber was emptied. Tarzan and Herkuf attempted to raise the trap door leading into Helen's cell; but it defied their every effort, even the Herculean strength of the Lord of the Jungle. And what was happening, or had happened, in the cell below?—cell or tomb?

And while Tarzan and Herkuf labored with the trap door a ptome awoke and sat up upon his hard bench, rubbing his eyes. He had had a strange, disquieting dream in which enemies had passed through the room of the ptomes. He looked about to see if anyone was there who should not be. Mechanically, he looked for his water suit and helmet. They were gone, and two other pegs were empty. Instantly he awoke his fellows and disclosed his discovery, telling them of his dream. They were all much perturbed, for such things had never happened before in the memory of man. They started to investigate immediately, going first to the throne room, where they soon discovered that two of the prisoners were missing.

"Herkuf is gone and the man called Tarzan," said one.

"But three suits and tridents were taken," pointed out another.

By this time the prisoners were awake; and they questioned them, with many threats; but they learned nothing for the prisoners knew nothing, and were quite as surprised as the ptomes.

"I have it!" cried a ptome at last. "It is quite plain that they have gone to the little chamber in the lake to release the girl, that is why they took he exra suit. Quick! Into your helmets! In the name of Atka, hurry!"

"We must not all go, or the rest of the prisoners may escape as the others did," suggested one; so only six of them donned their suits and hurried into the waters of Horus in pursuit of the two missing prisoners. Armed as they were, with tridents and knives, they had no thought but that they could easily overcome and recapture their quarry.

For many precious minutes the trap door refused to yield to the efforts of Tarzan and Herkuf; but at last it gave way, and they threw it open. Looking down into the darkness, they at first saw nothing; then Tarzan espied, dimly, a wan face apparently floating on the surface of the water. Were they, after all, too late? Was this the face of a dead girl?

Holding to the ladder and floating with her nose just above the water, Helen heard increasing sounds of activity just above her; then the trap door was lifted, and she saw two ptomes looking down at her. As they dragged her into the air chamber, she guessed that they had come to inflict some new torture.

They helped her to don the extra water suit, and led

146

her out of the air chamber into the lake. In their suits and helmets, she did not recognize them; and as there was no means of communication, she went on with them, ignorant of their identity, wondering what next Fate had in store for her.

As Herkuf led them away from the vicinity of the temple, the pursuing ptomes discovered them and hurried to overtake them. In the silence of the watery depths, no sound reached the ears of the fugitives; and they were ignorant of the danger approaching from behind; until, finally, Tarzan, always the wary jungle beast, looked back and saw the ptomes approaching. He touched Herkuf and Helen, and pointed; then he gathered them together, so that they all stood back to back to await the assault of the enemy he well knew they could not outdistance in flight. What the outcome of such a battle would be, he could not even guess. He knew that they were all unused to fighting in such a medium and with such weapons. A single rent in a suit might mean death by drowning, and doubtless their antagonists were adepts in the use of tridents. What he did not know was that the ptomes were as unused to underwater fighting as was he. Sometimes they had to defend themselves from the more dangerous denizens of the deep, but never had they been called upon to face human antagonists and weapons identical to their own.

So it was that Tarzan and Herkuf drew first blood; and now, for the first time, Helen realized that she might be in the hands of friends; yet that seemed entirely implausible, for how could she have friends among the ptomes?

With two of their number dead in the first encounter with the enemy, the four remaining ptomes became more wary. They circled cautiously, waiting for an opening; but there seemed no opening in the impregnable defense of the three, who could not be lured from the compact formation that presented a trident on every front. Suddenly one of the ptomes leaped above the heads of the quarry to attack them from a new angle; and as he did so, his fellows rushed in. But they rushed too close, and two of them went to their deaths on the tridents of Herkuf and Tarzan; then the one above them floated down and struck at the ape-man. As he did so, Helen jabbed suddenly upward with her trident, catching the fellow squarely in the chest. He wriggled horribly, like a speared fish, and then sank limply at her feet. The girl had to steel herself to keep from fainting.

With his fellows dead, the remaining ptome turned and fled toward the temple; but Tarzan dared not let him escape to bring reinforcements; so he pursued him, feeling like one in a bad dream, who makes strenuous efforts but accomplishes little or nothing. However, the ptome had the same watery medium to contend with; but not the giant muscles to overcome it that his pursuer possessed; so gradually Tarzan gained on him, while Herkuf and Helen followed in his wake.

When the ptome realized that he could not make good his escape, he turned at bay and prepared to fight; and Tarzan found him the most dangerous antagonist of all, for he was fighting with the desperation of a cornered rat. It was the strangest duel the ape-man had ever fought. The weird, mysterious silence of the depths; the grotesque medium that retarded his every movement; all baffled him. He was accustomed to fighting on one plane and not having antagonists leap above his head and thrust down at him, as the ptome suddenly did; but he fended the thrust, and seized his foe by the ankle. The ptome struggled to free himself, thrusting savagely with his trident; but at last Tarzan was sure of himself, as he dragged the lesser priest toward him.

At close quarters, the tridents were useless; and both men discarded them, each drawing his knife, the ptome slashing viciously but awkwardly at Tarzan, while the ape-man sought to seize the other's knife wrist; and while they fought, a large fish, swimming low, approached them; and Helen and Herkuf hurried up, like two hideous robots held back by an invisible hand.

Tarzan's fingers were touching the wrist of the ptome, he had almost succeeded in seizing the hand that held the dagger, when the great fish, frightened by the approach of Helen and Herkuf, darted past in an effort to escape, struck Tarzan's legs a heavy blow and upset him. As the ape-man fell backward, the ptome saw and seized his opportunity. He lunged forward upon the falling Tarzan, his knife ready to plunge into his foe's heart.

But once again Tarzan fended the weapon aside; and as he parried the blow, Helen and Herkuf reached him and plunged their tridents into the body of the ptome. As Tarzan floated to his feet, Helen wondered whose life it was she had helped to save and what his intentions toward her might be.

26

IN THE TEMPLE of Brulor all was confusion and excitement. Priests and warriors filled the throne room, investigating the mysterious disappearance of two prisoners. The locks of their cages were intact, and only d'Arnot guessed the truth as he noted a slight bend in two of the bars of Tarzan's cage.

"Once again there is hope," he whispered to Brian.

An excited ptome ran into the throne room; and, tearing off his helmet, hurried to the foot of Brulor's throne. "O Father of Diamonds," he cried, "I went to the little chamber in the lake. The woman is gone!"

"Gone? Where?" demanded Brulor.

"Who knows?" replied the ptome. "All that I know is that she is not there and that scattered over the bottom of Horus are the bodies of six ptomes, their water suits stripped from three. A demon is in our midst, O Father!"

Brulor leaped to his feet, trembling with rage. "They are not demons," he cried, "but mortal men who may die. One is that renegade, Herkuf; the other is the man called Tarzan. Whoever brings them to me, dead or alive, may name his own reward; but bring them alive if you can. Whoever profanes the temple of Brulor must die. So it is written."

And while Brulor raged, the objects of his wrath, led by Herkuf, were far out on the bottom of Horus. Having stripped the water suits from three of the dead ptomes, they had followed Herkuf, who was bent on leading them across the lake in accordance with the plan that he and

Tarzan had decided upon before their escape from the temple. Good fortune had given them possession of three extra water suits, which would fit in nicely with the plan they had in mind, a mad plan; but the only one that seemed at all likely to succeed.

As they approached deeper water, they descended into a valley of huge marine plants; and here they encountered the larger denizens of the deep; so that they were constantly compelled to fight off attacks, as monstrous, shadowy shapes glided about them. Mighty, grotesque plants waved their fronds above them in the dim light of the fading stars.

Helen was frankly terrified. She had no idea who these men were, nor where they were taking her, nor what their intentions toward her; and in addition to these, she did not see how they could escape the terrifying dangers that surrounded them, made doubly terrifying by the darkness and the strangeness of the scene. She felt that she could endure no more, and then a huge sea serpent swam from among the giant trees and rushed to attack them.

The men faced its horrible jaws with their puny tridents, while its long, sinous tail wreathed in spirals above them like a sentient Damoclean sword that might destroy them at any moment. Its protruding eyes glaring, its forked tongue darting from its fanged jaws, the serpent suddenly wrapped its tail about Helen and swam off. Instantly Tarzan dropped the extra water suit and helmet he had been carrying and sprang up in an effort to reach them, as Herkuf stood helpless on the lake bottom below.

Just by chance, the ape-man succeeded in seizing one of Helen's ankles; but he could not wrest her from the grip of that powerful tail. Slowly he drew himself up over the body of the girl in an effort to reach the body of the serpent. At the same time he tried to wrest her free; but the coils only tightened about her; and as the angry saurian turned and twisted, he had difficulty in holding on at all. It was only his great strength and agility that, despite his encumbering water suit, permitted him, finally, to climb to the monster's back. Again and again he drove his knife into the cold body, while Helen marvelled at the courage and strength of her unknown paladin.

Painfully, but not seriously wounded, the saurian

dropped the girl and turned upon the man-thing that dared thus to question its supremacy. Bleeding, hurt, infuriated, a creature of demoniacal fury, its one thought now was to destroy this rash thing that threatened its right to self-preservation. Fending off the jaws with his sharp knife that inflicted hurts which caused the serpent to recoil, Tarzan climbed steadily toward the great throat. Numa, the lion; Sheeta, the leopard; Wappi, the antelope; and man he had killed by severing the jugular. Why not this creature, too, in which blood flowed?

At last he reached his goal; and here, beneath the great throat, he found the tenderest skin his blade had yet pierced; and with a single stroke he severed the vein he had been seeking. There was a gush of blood, the creature writhed convulsively for a few moments; and then, as Tarzan slipped from its back, it turned belly up and floated away; while the ape-man sank gently toward the floor of the lake, where Helen stood, wide-eyed and wondering, looking up at him.

Dawn was breaking; and the increasing light made it possible for them to see to greater distances than before, and as Tarzan looked about for Herkuf, he saw him approaching, bringing along the water suit and helmet that Tarzan had discarded.

From this point on, the lake bottom rose steeply, taxing Helen's energies to such an extent that Tarzan had to help her for the remainder of the way to shore. Herkuf was not much better off than Helen, but he managed to stagger out of the water to fall exhausted on the bank. Only Tarzan seemed fresh and untired.

They lost no time in removing the uncomfortable helmets, and when Helen saw Tarzan's face she cried out in astonishment. "Tarzan!" she exclaimed. "But I might have known that it was you, for who else could have done for me what you have?"

"Paul," he said, with a smile.

"You're sweet," she said. "Oh, what a relief to feel safe once more. How wonderful to be alive after all that we have gone through, after that terrible chamber where they would have drowned me. I can't believe yet that I have escaped."

Close to shore, Herkuf had speared a fish; and now he

led them to a cave he knew of; and while Helen and Tarzan lay on the ground, he built a fire and broiled his catch.

"What are your plans?" Helen asked Tarzan.

"Herkuf knows where a boat is hidden on this side of the lake. We thought it safer to come here rather than to attempt to steal one from the quay at Ashair, knowing that after our escape was discovered there would be sentries everywhere. Tonight, we shall row across the lake; and Herkuf and I will go down in water suits and try to get past the ptomes again and bring out d'Arnot, Brian, and Lavac. That is why we took the three suits from the ptomes we killed. We were going to try to steal them from the ptomes' room. Now we won't have to go through that room, as we did before to steal suits, as Herkuf says there is a way around it."

"After we have eaten and rested," said Herkuf, "I'll go and see if the boat is still where I hid it. That was many years ago; but it was well hidden, and it is seldom that anyone comes to this part of the valley. I sank it in a tiny inlet beneath bushes that overhung the water."

"It has probably rotted away by this time," suggested Helen.

"No, I think not," replied Herkuf. "It would only rot if exposed to the air."

As they ate the broiled fish, they discussed their plans and recalled the adventures through which they had passed; and Helen asked Herkuf how it had been possible to construct the temple at the bottom of the lake. "That seems to me," she said, "an engineering feat far beyond the capabilities of the Asharians, for nothing else that they have accomplished, as far as I have seen, suggests more than a primitive knowledge of engineering. With the exception of these diving helmets, I have seen nothing that indicates great inventive genius, either."

"It was the invention of the diving helmet, coupled with a natural phenomenon, that made it possible to build the temple," explained Herkuf. "We are a very ancient race. We have occupied the valley of Tuen-Baka for perhaps three thousand years. Our origin is legendary, but it is believed that our early ancestors came down from the north, bringing with them a well developed civilization and considerable engineering knowledge. There were two factions or tribes. One settled at what is now Thobos, the other at Ashair. It was an Asharian who invented the diving helmet. He was always puttering around with metals and chemicals, trying to make gold from common substances; and during his experiments, he accidentally discovered a combination of chemicals that, when water was poured on them, generated air that could be breathed; but he had a sad end just as he was about to transmute a black powder he had compounded into gold. All that was necessary, he believed, was to apply great pressure suddenly; so he placed a little of it on a piece of lava and struck it with a hammer. There was a terrific noise and much smoke; and the roof blew off the inventor's house, and he went with it. One of his assistants, who miraculously escaped death, saw it all. But, though he did not succeed in making gold, he left behind him a great invention in the form of the diving helmet, which was thoroughly perfected and in common use, though more for sport than for any practical purpose."

"But what had that to do with the building of the temple?" asked Helen.

"I am coming to that. Off shore from Ashair, at the point above where the temple now stands, the water was always in constant turmoil, a jet of it often flying into the air fifty or a hundred feet with a great hissing sound. The origin of this phenomenon was a mystery which the Asharians would have liked to solve; so, one day, a venturesome youth donned a water suit and helmet and set forth on the bottom of the lake to investigate. He was gone about half an hour, when watchers on the shore saw him shoot up, above the surface of the water at the spot where the phenomenon occurred. By a miracle, he was not killed; and when he finally came back to shore, he reported that a great geyser of air was shooting up from a hole in the bottom of the lake.

"It was many years later that some one conceived the idea of building a temple around the air geyser to house the priesthood and holy of holies. Thousands of slaves were captured and set to cutting the lava blocks that were to form the temple walls. Innumerable water suits and helmets were made. The most difficult part of the work

153

was the capping of the air geyser, but this was finally accomplished; then the building of the temple commenced. It took a thousand years and cost twice that many lives. When it was completed and tightly sealed, it was, of course, entirely filled with water; but when the valve that had been installed in the geyser cap was opened, the water was forced out of the temple through a one-way valve. Today, the geyser furnishes pure air for the temple and actuates the doors of the air chambers."

"How wonderful!" commented Helen. "But where does this air supply come from?"

"It is, of course, mere conjecture," replied Herkuf; "but the theory is that during a great eruption, when Tuen-Baka was an active volcano, the entire top of the mountain was blown off and that when a great portion of it fell back into the crater it imprisoned a vast quantity of air, under great pressure, in a subterranean reservoir."

"And when that supply is exhausted?" inquired the girl.

Herkuf shrugged. "Horus will reclaim the temple. But there is yet a second theory. It is possible that there exists beneath the temple an immense deposit of the very chemicals that we use in our helmets, and that the trickling of water from the lake into this deposit is constantly generating fresh air."

"What a world of thought and labor and lives must have gone into the building of that structure!" exclaimed Helen, "and to what purpose? Why do men so waste their energies?"

"Does your race build no temples to its gods?" asked Herkuf.

27

MAGRA AND GREGORY halted on a rocky hillside above Ashair. The hot sun beat down upon them from a cloudless sky, the frowning walls of Tuen-Baka towered above them, below them stretched the calm waters of sacred Horus; and in the distance the entrance to the tunnel leading to the outer world beckoned to them and mocked them.

"Well, here we are," said Gregory. "This must be the secret entrance to the tunnel."

"Yes," said Magra, "we are here; but what now?"

"After what those poor devils told us," replied Gregory, "I think it would be foolish to throw our lives away uselessly by entering such a trap."

"I quite agree with you," said Magra. "We could accomplish nothing if we succeeded in getting into the temple. We'd only be captured and upset all of Tarzan's plans if he is successful in what he is attempting."

"What I can't understand," said Gregory, "is what has become of Helen, Brian, d'Arnot, and Lavac. Do you suppose they all went into the temple to help Tarzan?"

"They may have, or they may all have been recaptured. About all we can do is wait."

"Suppose we go on below Ashair and look for a hiding place. If we are between Ashair and the entrance to the tunnel, they will have to pass us to get out of the valley, for there is no other way out, so far as I know."

"I think you are right," agreed Gregory, "but I wonder if it will be safe to try to pass Ashair in the day time."

"Just as safe as it is to remain here at the mouth of this secret passage to their temple. Some of the Asharians may stumble upon us here at any time."

"All right," said Gregory, "let's try it. There are quantities of enormous lava blocks farther up at the foot of the escarpment. We may be able to make our way past the city and be entirely screened from it by them."

"Let's go," said Magra.

They made the laborious ascent to the jumbled pile of lava that had fallen from above; and though the going was rough, they found that they were entirely hidden from the city; and eventually came down again close to the lake well beyond Ashair.

Between them and the lake a low, limestone ridge shut off their view of the water. It paralleled the shore line, and extended for about a quarter of a mile, falling gradually to the level of the surrounding land. Upon its summit shrubs grew sparsely and a few gnarled trees. A rise of land hid it from Ashair.

"Look!" said Magra, pointing. "Isn't that a cave?"

"It looks like one," replied Gregory. "We'll have a look at it. If it's habitable, we're in luck, for we can hide there and keep a lookout for the others from the summit of the ridge."

"How about food?" asked Magra.

"I imagine we can find fruit and nuts in some of those larger trees just below the ridge," replied Gregory, "and if I have any luck at all I should be able to get a fish now and then."

As they talked, they approached the entrance to the cave, which, from the outside, appeared to be perfectly adapted to their needs; but they entered it cautiously. For a short distance only was the interior visible in the dim light that came through the entrance; beyond that they could see nothing.

"I think I'll explore a little before we settle down to light housekeeping," said Gregory.

"I'll go with you."

The cave narrowed into a dark corridor, which they followed, gropingly, in almost total darkness; but at a sharp turn it became lighter, and presently they came into a large cavern into which the sun poured through an opening in the roof. The cavern was large and grotesquely beautiful. Stalactites of various hues depended from ceiling and walls, while strangely shaped stalagmites covered much of the floor. Erosion had wrought strange limestone figures which rose like the creations of some mad sculptor among the tinted stalagmites.

"What a gorgeous spectacle!" exclaimed Magra.

"It is marvellous, and the coloring is beautiful," agreed Gregory, "but I think we should explore a little farther to make certain that it is a safe place for us to hide."

"Yes," said Magra, "you're quite right. There's an opening there at the far end of the cavern that may lead to something else. Let's have a look at it."

They found that the opening led into another corridor, dark and tortuous; and as they felt their way along it, Magra shuddered.

156

"There is something uncanny about this place," she whispered.

"Nonsense," said Gregory. "That's just because it's dark in here. Women don't like the dark."

"Do you?" she asked.

"Well, no; but just because a place is dark doesn't mean that it's dangerous."

"But," she insisted, "I have a feeling that we are being watched by unseen eyes."

"Oh, that's just your imagination, my dear child," laughed Gregory. "Your nerves are unstrung; and I don't wonder, after all that you have gone through. It's surprising that we're not all nervous wrecks."

"I don't believe that it's imagination," replied Magra. "I tell you I can feel that we are not alone. Something is near us. Something is watching us. Let's go back and get out of this terrible place. It's evil. I know it."

"Try and calm yourself, my dear," soothed Gregory; "there's no one near us; and anyway, if the place is evil, we want to know it."

"I hope you're right," said Magra; "but I'm still terrified; and, as you know, I'm not easily frightened. Here's an opening in the wall. It may be another corridor. Which one had we better take?"

"I think we'll keep right on in this one," replied Gregory. "It seems to be the main corridor. If we start turning off, we may become lost. I've heard of people being lost down in caves in Kentucky or Virginia or somewhere, and never being found again.

Just then a hand seized Magra from behind and whisked her through the opening they had just passed. Gregory heard a single piercing scream behind him, and wheeled about. To his horror, he found that he was alone. Magra had disappeared. He called her name aloud, but there was no reply; then he turned to go back and search for her. As he did so, another hand reached out from an opening on the opposite side of the corridor and seized him. He struggled and fought; but all his efforts were futile, and he was dragged into the darkness of a side corridor.

Magra, too, had fought for her liberty; but uselessly. The powerful creature that had seized her, dragged her along the dark corridor in silence. She did not know whether she were in the clutches of a man or a beast. After her experience with Ungo, it was only natural that she might have been in doubt.

The corridor was not long, and presently it ended in a second large cavern. It was then that she saw that her captor was a white robed figure with hooded face. She saw the bare hands; and knew that it was no ape that had seized her, but a man. There were a number of others like him in the cavern, in the center of which was a pool of water.

At the far end of the cavern a throne stood upon a dais; and before the throne was an altar, while directly behind it was an opening, roughly arched, looking out upon the lake, which was almost on a level with the floor of the cavern. The cavern was beautiful; but the whole scene was given a weird aspect by the presence of the sinister, silent, white robed figures that stood staring at her through dimly seen eyes that shown through slits in their hoods.

Magra had scarcely more than taken in the scene before her when she saw Gregory being dragged in as she had been. They looked at one another resignedly, and Gregory shook his head. "Guess we're in for it," he said. "Looks like the Klu Klux Klan. You were right. Some of them must have been watching us."

"I wonder what they are," she said, "and what they want of us. God! Haven't we been through enough, without this?"

"I don't wonder Tuen-Baka is taboo and Ashair forbidden. If I ever get out of it, it will be taboo as far as I am concerned."

"If we ever get out," she said rather wistfully.

"We got out of Thobos," he reminded her.

"Yes, I know; but we have no Tarzan nor any Thetan here. Now we are on our own, and we are helpless."

"Maybe they don't intend us any harm," he suggested. "If I only knew their language, I'd ask 'em. They have a

158

language. They've been whispering together ever since they brought us in."

"Try Swahili," she suggested. "Every one else we've seen in this accursed country speaks it."

"My Swahili is a little lame," he said, "but if they understand Swahili maybe they can make it out." He turned toward the nearest white robed figure, and cleared his throat. "Why did you bring us here?" he asked. "What are you going to do with us? We haven't done anything to you."

"You dared enter the temple of the true god," replied the man. "Who are you to dare enter the sacred temple of Chon?"

"They are minions of Atka," said another.

"Or spies of the false Brulor," suggested a third.

"We are nothing of the kind," said Magra. "We are just strangers who became lost. All we want to do is find our way out of Tuen-Baka."

"Then why did you come here?"

"We were looking for a place to hide until we could get out," replied the girl.

"You are probably lying. We shall keep you here until the true god returns; then you shall learn your fate and the manner of your death."

28

AFTER THEY HAD rested, Herkuf, Helen, and Tarzan went to look for the boat that Herkuf had hidden, in which they were to return to the temple of Brulor in an attempt to rescue d'Arnot, Brian, and Lavac. The inlet in which he had sunk it was not a great distance from the cave they had chosen; and as almost the entire distance was through wooded country, they had no fear of being detected by the occupants of any of the Asharian galleys which occasionally passed within eyesight of the shore, as they patrolled the lower end of Horus in eternal quest of their hereditary enemies from Thobos.

When they reached the inlet, Herkuf parted the overhanging bushes and looked down into the shallow water. "This is the place," he muttered to himself. "I know it is the place. I cannot be mistaken."

"What's wrong?" asked Tarzan. "Can't you find it?"

"This is the place," repeated Herkuf, "but the boat is not here. Though I hid it carefully, some one found it. Now all our plans are wrecked. What are we to do?"

"Can't we walk around the end of the lake and enter the water near the temple from the Asharian shore?" asked Helen.

"The escarpment at the lower end of the lake is unscalable," replied Herkuf. "If we went by way of Thobos, we should most certainly be captured; and although I was once a priest of Chon at Thobos, no one would know me now; and we should all be imprisoned."

"Maybe we could build a raft," suggested the girl.

Herkuf shook his head. "We have no tools," he said; "and even if we had, we'd never dare attempt it, as the Asharians would be sure to discover us."

"Must we give up, then?" demanded Helen. "Oh, we can't do that and leave Paul and Brian and Lavac to die."

"There is a way," said Tarzan.

"What is it?" demanded Herkuf.

"When it is dark, I'll swim to Ashair and steal a boat from the quay there."

"That is impossible," said Herkuf. "You saw with what we had to contend when we crossed last night. You wouldn't get half way across, swimming at the surface. We'd better walk back."

"It was only by the best of luck that we got across last night," Tarzan reminded him. "We might not be so lucky another time; and, if we did succeed, we should still be without a boat to return to Thobos or escape through the tunnel. You know that the success of our whole plan rested upon our having a boat. I shall swim the lake to-night."

160

"Don't do it, Tarzan; please don't," begged Helen. "You would just be throwing your life away uselessly."

"I do not intend to throw my life away at all," he replied. "I have my knife."

They returned to the cave to await darkness; and, finding it impossible to dissuade Tarzan from his plan, Herkuf and Helen finally gave up in despair; and, when darkness fell, they stood at the shore line and watched him wade into the dark waters of Horus. With straining eyes they watched his progress until he disappeared from their view in the darkness, and even then they remained where they were, staring out into the black void across the blacker waters.

Tarzan had completed about half the distance to the Asharian shore without encountering any dangers, when he saw a torch flare suddenly in the bow of a galley only a short distance from him. He watched it; and when it altered its course and came toward him, he realized that he had been discovered. To be taken now by an Asharian galley would doubtless mean death not only for him but for the men he was risking his life to save, and so he grasped at the only chance he had to elude them. Diving, he swam away, trying to escape the circle of their torch's light; and, glancing back, he felt that he might succeed, for the light appeared to be receding; but as he rose toward the surface for air before diving again, he saw a shadowy form approaching him; and knew that at last the thing that Helen and Herkuf had so feared had happened. He recalled his words of assurance to them, "I have my knife," and half smiled as he drew it.

On Ashair's distant wall, a sentry saw the flare of the torch out upon the lake and summoned an officer. "A galley from Thobos," he said, "for there are no Asharian galleys out tonight."

The officer nodded. "I wonder why they risked a light," he said. "They always sneak by in the night without torches. Well, it is our good luck, and because of it we shall have a prize tonight and some more victims for Atka and Brulor."

As the great shark turned on its back to seize Tarzan,

he plunged his knife into its belly and ripped it open for a distance of several feet. Mortally hurt, the great fish thrashed about in its agony, dyeing the water crimson with its blood and creating a great commotion upon the surface of the lake, a commotion that attracted the attention of those in the galley.

The ape-man, avoiding the lashing tail and angry jaws of the shark, now saw other great forms converging upon them, silent, sinister tigers of the deep attracted at first, like their fellow, by the light of the torch in the bow of the galley; but now by the blood of the wounded shark. Terrible creatures, they were coming for the kill.

His lungs bursting, Tarzan swam toward the surface for air, confident that the wounded shark would occupy the attention of the others. He knew, from the radiance of the water, that he would come up close to the galley; but he had to choose between that and death from drowning; there was no other alternative.

As he broke the surface of the water, he was close beside the galley; and warriors seized him and drew him over the gunwale. Here now was an end to all the fine plans he and Herkuf had concocted, for to fall into the hands of the Asharians must be equivalent to the signing of his death warrant; but as he looked at his captors he saw the black plumes of Thobos and heard a familiar voice call him by name. It was Thetan's.

"We were sneaking past Ashair without lights," he said, "on our way down river to capture a few slaves; but what in the world were you doing out here in the middle of Horus?"

"I was swimming to Ashair to steal a boat," replied the ape-man.

"Are you crazy?" demanded Thetan. "No man could hope to live in these waters. Why, they are alive with flesh eaters."

"So I discovered, but I think I should have gotten through. I must have been half way across. It was not my life that was at stake, Thetan, but those of my friends who are prisoners in Ashair. I must reach Ashair and get a boat."

Thetan thought for a moment; then he said, "I'll take you. I can land you on the shore below the city, but I advise you to give up all thought of it. You cannot enter Ashair without being discovered, and that will be the end of you."

"I don't want to go ashore," replied Tarzan. "I have two companions across the lake from the city. If you will take the three of us to a point above the temple of Brulor, I won't have to go ashore and steal a boat."

"What good will that do you?" demanded Thetan.

"We have water suits and helmets. We are going into the temple to get our friends, and I've got to take Brulor and The Father of Diamonds to Herat to get him to release Magra and Gregory."

"They've already escaped," said Thetan, "and Herat is furious." He did not say that he had helped them, as other Thobotian warriors were listening.

"That really doesn't make much difference," said Tarzan. "We can't escape from Tuen-Baka without Herat's aid. We'll need a galley and provisions. If I bring Brulor and The Father of Diamonds to him, he'll give us what we need, I'm sure."

"Yes," agreed Thetan, "but you won't ever bring Brulor and The Father of Diamonds to Herat. What chance have you, practically unaided, to do what we have been trying to do for years?"

Trazan shrugged. "I still must try," he said. "Will you help me?"

"If I can't dissuade you, I'll help you. Where are your friends?"

Tarzan pointed in the general direction of the cave where he had left Helen and Herkuf, the torch was extinguished, and the galley's nose turned toward the shore.

From the quay at Ashair, six galleys put out without lights into the darkness of the night to search for the quarry, which they could no longer see since the torch had been extinguished; and as they rowed from shore, they fanned out, some up river, some down, to cover the most territory in their search.

The shore line ahead of the galley bearing Tarzan was a long, black silhouette against the night sky. No landmarks were visible; and the shore was a straight, black line without breaks or indentations. Only the merest chance might bring them to the spot where Helen and Herkuf waited. When they were quite close to shore, Tarzan called Herkuf's name in a low voice; and immediately there came an answering hail from their right. A few minutes later the keel of the galley touched gravel a few yards from shore, and Tarzan leaped out and waded to where Helen and Herkuf stood. They were amazed that he had returned so soon, amazed that he had returned at all, for they had seen the torchlit galley and believed that he had been captured by Asharians.

Briefly he explained what had occurred; and, telling Herkuf to follow with the water suits and helmets and weapons, he tossed Helen to a shoulder and waded back to the galley, which turned its nose toward Ashair as soon as Herkuf was aboard. Tarzan, Helen, and Herkuf immediately donned their water suits, leaving their helmets off, temporarily, so that they could talk.

Silently, the galley glided out into the lake, the oars dipping without noise as they were plied by thirty well trained slaves, who had learned by long experience the necessity for stealth in passing through the lower waters of Horus where Asharian galleys might be lying in wait for them—Asharian galleys and Asharian warriors who might send them to the bottom chained to their thwarts.

About mid-lake a torch suddenly burst into flame to the right of them; then another to the left, and in quck succession four more between them, forming a semi-circle toward the center of which they were moving. With the lighting of the torches, a loud Asharian war cry broke the deathly stillness of the night; and the Asharian galleys moved to encircle that of Thetan.

Nothing but immediate flight might save the Thobotians; and as the prow of the galley turned quickly toward the lower end of the lake in an effort to elude the jaws of the closing circle of enemy galleys, Tarzan called to Helen and Herkuf to don their helmets as he adjusted his own; then, seizing Helen's hand and signalling Herkuf to follow, he leaped overboard with the girl, while Thetan urged his slaves to greater speed.

29

H AND IN HAND, Tarzan and Helen sank gently down
to the darkness of the lake's bottom. If Herkuf were
near them, they could see nothing of him; and so
Tarzan waited for the coming of the new day that would
lift the black veil from the mysteries of Horus's depths,
as to proceed without Herkuf might easily foredoom the
entire venture to failure. That they might never find him,
Tarzan was aware; but he could only wait and hope.

It was an eerie experience for Helen Gregory that was
rendered doubly trying by the recollection of her previous experiences in this silent world of horrors. Dimly
seen, great forms glided through the forest of grotesque
treelike plants that waved their dark foliage on every
hand. Momentarily, the girl expected some hideous monster to attack; but the night passed and dawn broke without their having once been threatened. It seemed a miracle
to her, but the explanation probably lay in the fact
that they had remained quietly sitting on the gravelly bottom. Had they been moving, it might have been different.

As the light of the new day filtered down to them,
Tarzan looked about for Herkuf; but he was nowhere to
be seen. Reluctantly, the ape-man started off across the
lake toward the temple of Brulor. What he could accomplish alone, he did not know, as part of the plan was to
enter the temple during a period of meditation and release
the prisoners; but of the three, only Herkuf was familiar
with the mechanism that operated the doors to the air
chamber and emptied and refilled it; only Herkuf knew the
exact time of the periods of meditation.

Unable to communicate with Tarzan, Helen followed
where he led, ignorant of his new plans but more secure
in her faith in him than he was of himself in this particular
venture, where every condition varied so from all that he

had been accustomed to meet in the familiar jungles that he knew so well.

They had gone but a short distance in the direction in which Tarzan thought the temple lay, when they came upon Herkuf. He, too, had been waiting for daylight, feeling certain that Tarzan would have done the same and that, having leaped overboard almost simultaneously, they could not be far separated. It was with feelings of the greatest relief that they found themselves reunited.

Herkuf took the lead now, and with Tarzan and Helen following, commenced the tiresome and dangerous journey toward Ashair, all of them now greatly encouraged after the long hours of doubt and uncertainty.

They had not gone far when they came upon the wreck of a large galley partly embedded in the sand. That it had been there for years was attested by the size of the marine growth which had sprouted through its ribs, entwining the skeletons of its slaves still lying in their rusted chains.

Herkuf evinced considerable excitement; and, motioning them to wait, clambered into the interior of the craft, from which he presently emerged carrying a splendid jeweled casket. That he was overcome by excitement was obvious, but hampered by his helmet he could only express it by waving the casket before their faces and dancing jubilantly. What it was he had recovered, they could not guess, unless it were that the casket contained treasure of fabulous worth.

At last, and without further adventure, they approached the temple of Brulor; and here they went cautiously, seeking the shelter of the trees and plants that grew in the gardens of the ptomes, moving stealthily from one to another, each time assuring themselves that no ptome was in sight, knowing that at any moment one might emerge from the air chamber that they could now see. Approaching the temple, they found a place where they could hide concealed from the gardens and the air chamber door. Here they must wait until Herkuf signalled that the time had arrived when it might be safe to enter the temple. How long that would be only he could guess with any degree of accuracy. Near them was a window through which they could have looked into the temple had they dared; but as long as it was light outside they could not take the risk; and so they waited, tired, hungry, and thirsty; waited for night to fall.

Inside the temple the caged prisoners were gnawing on their evening meal of raw fish. Atan Thome enlarged in glowing terms upon his plans when he should come into possession of The Father of Diamonds and dazzle the world with his wealth. Lal Taask, scowling, cursed him. Akamen brooded in silence upon his lost liberty and his vanished dream of power. Brian and d'Arnot spoke together in low tones. Lavac paced his cage like a captive polar bear.

"I think your friend, Tarzan, has run off and left us," remarked Brian.

"You think that because you don't know him as well as I do," replied d'Arnot. "As long as he and we live he will try to rescue us."

"He will have to be a super-man to do it," said Brian.

"He is—that and all of that. He may fail, of course, but he will come nearer succeeding than any man who lives."

"Well, anyway, he got Helen out of that torture chamber they'd put her in," said Brian. "Wasn't old Brulor sore, though! Of course he really hasn't had time to get her to a place of safety and come back for us; but every minute is an hour in here, and so it seems like a very long time since he went away. Did you know he was going?"

"Yes; he told me; but I didn't know when he and Herkuf left. I was asleep. I am sure he must have gotten her out; otherwise he'd have been back after us."

"Unless he was killed," suggested Brian. "Anyway we know he took her out. That was what old Brulor was raving about."

"I mean out of the lake—to some place of safety. Sometimes I think I'll go crazy if I don't know."

"We've got one nut here now," said Brian, nodding toward Atan Thome. "We couldn't stand another. Anyway, wait until you've been here as long as I have; then you'll really have an excuse to go cuckoo."

"They're all clearing out of the throne room now," said d'Arnot. "The period of meditation has come. I wonder what they meditate about."

"Meditate, hell!" exclaimed Brian. "Ask the handmaidens."

Outside the temple the weary trio waited. Since the evening before they had had neither food nor water, nor spoken a single word; but now Herkuf cautiously moved to a spot opposite the window but not too close to it. It was dark now, and there was little danger that he would be seen from the inside. The throne room was deserted except for the prisoners. He came back to Tarzan and Helen and nodded that all was right; then he left the casket at Helen's feet and motioned that she was to remain where she was. She was very lonely after Tarzan and Herkuf left her.

This was the moment for which the two men had been waiting. What did it hold for them? Carrying out the plan they had carefully laid out in every detail, the two men each speared a fish; then, with their quarry wriggling on their tridents, they went to the air chamber. It was only a matter of a few moments before they had passed through it and stood in the corridor leading to the ptomes' room.

Beside them was another door opening into a passageway that led to the throne room, avoiding the ptomes' room. Herkuf tried to open it, but could not. He shrugged. There was nothing to do now but make the attempt to pass through the room where the ptomes should be sleeping. They prayed that they were sleeping. Cautiously, Herkuf opened the door to that room and looked in; then he beckoned Tarzan to follow him.

The entire success of their venture depended upon their reaching the throne room unchallenged. They had almost succeeded, when a ptome, awakening, sat up and looked at them. With their fish upon their tridents, the two men continued on unconcernedly across the room. The sleepy ptome, scarce awake, thought them two of his own kind, and lay down to sleep again. Thus they came in safety to the throne room, while outside, Helen waited in the loneliness of the black water. She was almost happy, so certain was she that Tarzan and Herkuf would succeed in liberating d'Arnot, Brian, and Lavac; but then she was not aware of the figure in a white water suit that was swimming down toward her from above and behind. Whatever it was, it was evident that it had discovered her and was swimming directly toward her.

Tarzan and Herkuf hurried directly to the cages, tossing their fish to the floor. The excited prisoners watched them, for they had never seen ptomes behave like this. Only d'Arnot really guessed who they were. Seizing the bars in his powerful grasp, Tarzan released them one after the other, cautioning them to silence with a gesture; then he removed his helmet and told d'Arnot, Brian, and Lavac to put on the three water suits that Herkuf carried.

"The rest of you," he said, "may be able to escape by the secret passage at the end of the long corridor. Does any of you know where to find it and open it?"

"I do," replied Akamen.

"So do I," said Atan Thome. "I learned from Akamen." As he spoke he darted toward the altar and seized the casket containing The Father of Diamonds, the accursed casket that had wrought such havoc.

As Helen felt a hand seize her from behind, she turned to see the strange figure in white confronting her; and her vision of a successful termination of their venture faded. Once again she was plunged into the depths of despair. She tried to wrench herself free from the restraining hand, but she was helpless to escape. She realized that she must not be taken now, for it might jeopardize the lives and liberty of all her companions; she knew that they would search for her and that the delay might prove fatal to them. A sudden rage seized her; and, wheeling, she tried to drive her trident into the heart of her captor. But the creature that held her was alert and powerful. It wrenched the trident from her hands and cast it aside; then it seized her by a wrist and swam up with her toward the surface of the lake. The girl still struggled, but she was helpless. To what new and unpredictable fate was she being dragged? Who, now, might find or save her?

In the throne room of the temple, Tarzan and Herkuf saw all their efforts, their risks, and their plans being brought to nothing by the stupid avarice of three men, for as Atan Thome had seized the casket, Lal Taask and Brian Gregory had leaped upon him; and the three were fighting for the vast treasure for which they had risked their lives. At sight of the casket in the hands of another, Brian had forgotten all his fine resolutions; and cupidity dominated him to the exclusion of all else.

Tarzan ran forward to quiet them, but they thought that he too wanted the casket; so they fought down the throne room in an effort to evade him; and then that happened which Tarzan had feared—a door burst open and a horde of ptomes poured into the throne room. They wore no encumbering water suits or helmets, but they carried tridents and knives. Tarzan, Herkuf, and the liberated prisoners waited to receive them. Brian and Lal Taask, realizing that here was a matter of life and death, abandoned the casket temporarily to assist in the attempt to repulse the ptomes; but Atan Thome clung desperately to his treasure, and sneaking stealthily behind the others he made for the corridor at the far end of which was the entrance to the secret passageway that led to the rocky hillside above Ashair.

It devolved upon Tarzan to bear the brunt of the battle with the ptomes. Beside him, only Herkuf was armed; and the others fought with their bare hands but with such desperation that the ptomes fell back, while Tarzan speared them on his trident and tossed them among their fellows.

It was upon this scene that Brulor burst, red of face and trembling with rage; then above the yells and curses of the battling men there rose his screaming voice as he stood behind the empty altar.

"Curses!" he cried. "Curses upon the profaners of the temple! Death to them! Death to him who hath raped the casket of The Father of Diamonds! Summon the warriors of Ashair to avenge the sacrilege!"

Herkuf saw his Nemesis standing defenseless before him, and he saw red with the pent up hatred of many years. He leaped to the dais, and Brulor backed away, screaming for help; but the ptomes who remained alive were too busily engaged now, for all the prisoners who remained had armed themselves with the tridents and knives of the ptomes who had fallen.

"Die, imposter!" screamed Herkuf. "For years I have lived in the hope of this moment. Let the warriors of Ashair come, for now I may die happy. The true god shall

170

be avenged and the wrong you did me wiped out in your blood."

Brulor dropped to his knees and begged for mercy; but there was no mercy in the heart of Herkuf, as he raised his trident and drove it with both hands deep into the heart of the terrified man grovelling before him. Thus died Brulor, the false god.

A breathless ptome had staggered into the presence of Atka, who sat among her nobles at a great banquet. "What is the meaning of this?" demanded the Queen.

"Oh, Atka," cried the lesser priest. "The prisoners have been liberated and they are killing the ptomes. Send many warriors at once or they will all be slain."

Atka could not conceive of such a thing transpiring in the throne room of the temple of Brulor, yet she realized that the man was in earnest; so she gave orders that warriors were to be sent at once to quell the disturbance.

"They will soon bring order," she said, and returned to her feasting.

When the last ptome had fallen, Tarzan saw that Akamen was dead and that Taask and Thome had disappeared with the casket. "Let them go," he said. "The Father of Diamonds is bad luck."

"Not I," said Brian. "I shan't let them go. Why do you suppose I have suffered in this hell-hole? Now I have a chance to reap my reward; and when others steal it, you say, 'let them go.' "

Tarzan shrugged. "Do as you please," he said; then he turned to the others. "Come, we must get out of here before they get a chance to send a lot of warriors down on top of us."

All four were now in their water suits, and were adjusting their helmets as they made their way toward the corridor that led to the water chamber. Brian had reached the end of the throne room. He was the first to realize that the warriors of Ashair were already upon them. Throwing himself to the floor, he feigned death as the warriors rushed past him into the throne room.

When the others saw them, they thought that they were lost; but Herkuf motioned them to follow him, as he hurried on toward the air chamber. Tarzan had no idea what Herkuf planned to do. He only knew that there would not be time to pass through the air chamber before the warriors reached it and reversed the valves; then they would be caught like rats in a trap. He had no intention of inviting any such situation. He would turn his back to the wall and fight. Maybe he could delay the warriors long enough for the others to escape. That was what he thought; so he turned at the doorway leading from the throne room, and took his stand. The others, glancing back, saw what he was doing. D'Arnot took his place beside him, ignoring the ape-man's attempt to motion him on. Herkuf ran rapidly toward the air chamber. Lavac could have followed him to safety, but instead he took his stand beside d'Arnot in the face of certain death.

While Herkuf hastened on toward the air chamber, the warriors hesitated in the throne room, appalled by the bloody shambles that met their astonished view and confused by the fact that the three who faced them appeared to be ptomes of the temple; but at last, seeing no other enemy, the officer in charge of Atka's warriors ordered them forward; while out of sight, Herkuf worked feverishly with the controls of the air chamber, spinning valve handles and pulling levers.

Shouting now, the warriors came steadily down the length of the throne room toward the forlorn hope making a last stand before over-whelming odds; and the warriors looked for an easy victory. Nor were they alone in this belief, which was shared by the three who opposed them.

As the warriors closed upon the three, Tarzan met the leader in a duel between spear and trident, while d'Arnot and Lavac stood upon either side of him, determined, as was the ape-man, to sell their lives dearly; and as they fought thus, there was a sudden rush of water through the doorway behind them.

Herkuf had thought and acted quickly in the emergency that had confronted them, taking advantage of the only means whereby he and his companions could be saved from the vengeance of the warriors. Throwing open both doors of the air chamber, he had let the waters of Horus pour in to fill the temple.

Safe in their water suits, Tarzan, d'Arnot, and Lavac

watched the gushing torrent drive back their foes, as, cursing and yelling, the warriors of Ashair sought to climb over one another in their mad panic to escape the watery death Herkuf had loosed upon them out of sacred Horus; but not one escaped as the water filled the throne room and rose through the upper chambers of the temple. It was a gruesome sight from which the three turned gladly at a signal from Tarzan and followed him toward the air chamber, beyond which he had left Helen waiting in the garden of the ptomes.

30

U P AND UP through the waters of Horus, Helen was dragged by the ghostly figure until, at last, they reached the precipitous cliff, the summit of which forms the coast line near Ashair. Here the creature dragged his captive into the mouth of a dark cavern, a den of horror to the frightened girl.

Magra and Gregory had been held captives in the cavern for a night and a day waiting for the return of the true god, Chon, who was to decide their fate. They had not been ill treated; and they had been given food, but always there was the feeling of menace. It was in the air, in the strange garmenture of their captors, in their whisperings and in their silences. It affected both Magra and Gregory similarly, leaving them blue and despondent.

They were sitting beside the pool in the center of the cavern almost exactly twenty-four hours after their capture, the white robed figures crouching around them, when there was a sudden breaking of the still surface of the water and two grotesque diving helmets appeared, one white, the other dark.

"The true god has returned," cried one of the priests.

"Now the strangers shall be judged, and punishment meted out to them."

As the two figures emerged from the pool and removed their helmets, Magra and Gregory gasped in astonishment.

"Helen!" cried the latter. "Thank God that you still live. I had given you up for dead."

"Father!" exclaimed the girl. "What are you doing here? Tarzan told us that you and Magra were prisoners in Thobos."

"We escaped," said Magra, "but perhaps we would have been better off there. God only knows what we face here."

The figure in white that had emerged with Helen proved, when he removed his helmet, to be an old man with a bushy white beard. He looked at Helen in astonishment.

"A girl!" he cried. "Since when has false Brulor made ptomes of girls?"

"I am not a ptome," replied Helen. "I was a prisoner of Brulor, and adopted this method to escape."

"Perhaps she lies," said a priest.

"If these be enemies," said the old man, "I shall know when I consult the oracle in the entrails of the man. If they be not enemies, the girls shall become my handmaidens; but if they be, they shall die as the man dies, on the altar of the true god Chon and lost Father of Diamonds."

"And if you find that we are not enemies," demanded Magra, "what good will that do this man, whom you will have already killed? We tell you that we are friends, meaning you no harm. Who are you to say that we are not? Who are you to kill this good man?" Her voice was vibrant with just anger.

"Silence, woman!" commanded a priest. "You are speaking to Chon, the true god."

"If he were any sort of a god at all," snapped Magra, "he would know that we are not enemies. He would not have cut up an innocent man and ask questions of his entrails."

"You do not understand," said Chon, indulgently. "If the man is innocent and has told the truth, he will not die

174

when I remove his entrails. If he dies, that will prove his guilt."

Magra stamped her foot. "You are no god at all," she cried. "You are just a wicked old sadist."

Several priests sprang forward threateningly, but Chon stopped them with a gesture. "Do not harm her," he said; "she knows not what she says. When we have taught her to know the truth, she will be contrite. I am sure that she will become a worthy handmaiden, for she has loyalty and great courage. Treat them all well while they are among us waiting for the hour of inquisition."

* * *

Atan Thome fled upward along the secret passageway from the temple of Brulor, hugging the precious casket to his breast; and behind him came Lal Taask, his mind aflame with what was now the one obsession of his life—the killing of his erstwhile master. Secondary to that was his desire to possess the great diamond which reposed in the jeweled casket. Ahead of him he could hear the screams and jibberings of the madman, which served to inflame his rage still further. And behind them both came Brian Gregory, all his fine resolutions forgotten now that The Father of Diamonds seemed almost within his grasp. He knew that he might have to commit murder to obtain it; but that did not deter him in the least, for his avarice, like that of many men, bordered almost upon madness.

Out into the open and along the rocky hillside fled Atan Thome. When Lal Taask reached the open, he saw his quarry scarce a hundred yards ahead of him. Other eyes saw them both, the eyes of Ungo the great bull ape, which, with his fellows, hunted for lizards among the great rocks farther up the hillside. The sight of the two men, the screaming of Atan Thome, excited him. He recalled that Tarzan had told him that they must not attack men unless he were attacked; but there had been no interdiction against joining in their play, and this looked like play to Ungo. It was thus that playful apes chased one another. Of course, Ungo was a little old for play, being a sullen, surly old bull; but he was still imitative, and what the tarmangani did, he desired to do. His fellows were imbued with the same urge toward emulation.

As Brian Gregory came out into the open from the mouth of the secret passageway, he saw the great apes, jabbering with excitement, bounding down the hillside toward Atan Thome and the pursuing Lal Taask. He saw the men stop and then turn and flee in terror from the mighty beast-men charging down upon them.

For the moment Lal Taask discarded all thoughts of vengeance, as the first law of Nature dominated and directed him; but Atan Thome clung tenaciously to his precious casket. Ungo was delighted with this new game, as he came bounding after the fleeing, screaming Thome, whom he easily overtook. The man, thinking that death was upon him, tried to beat off the ape with one hand while he clung tightly to the casket with the other; that, he would not give up, even in death. Killing, however, was not in the mind of the anthropoid. It was the game in which he was interested; so he snatched the casket from the screaming man as easily as one man takes another's wife in Hollywood, and went bounding off, hoping that some one would pursue him that the game might continue.

Lal Taask, running away, glanced back over his shoulder to see his dream of riches irremediably shattered, leaving nothing now in life for him but his hatred of Atan Thome and his desire for vengeance. Furious with hate and thwarted avarice, he ran back to Thome to wreak his final revenge, barehanded, upon the screaming maniac. Lal Taask was choking and beating Atan Thome when Brian Gregory reached them and dragged the infuriated Indian from his victim. "What are you fools thinking of?" he demanded. "You're making enough noise to attract every warrior in Ashair. I ought to kill both of you; but right now we've got to forget all of that and work together to escape, for we'll never see that casket again."

Lal Taask knew that Gregory was right, but Atan Thome knew nothing. He could only think of The Father of Diamonds which he had lost, and impelled by a new maniacal impulse he suddenly broke away from Brian and ran screaming in the direction in which Ungo had disappeared with the casket. Lal Taask started after him, a curse upon his lips; but Brian layed a detaining hand on the man's arm.

"Let him go," he said; "he'll never get the casket from Ungo—he'll probably get himself killed instead. That accursed casket! So many have suffered and died because of it, and that poor fool has gone mad."

"Perhaps he is the most fortunate of all," said Lal Taask.

"I wish that I had never heard of it," continued Brian. "I have lost my father and sister, and probably all of their friends are dead because of my greed. A moment ago I would still have risked my life for it, but the sight of that jibbering idiot has brought me to my senses. I wouldn't have the thing now; I am not superstitious, but I believe there is a curse on it."

"Perhaps you are right," said Lal Taask. "I do not care so much about the casket as I did about killing that mad devil, but the gods have willed it otherwise. I shall have to be content."

Apelike, Ungo soon tired of his new bauble; and tossed the casket carelessly to the ground, his thoughts reverting to the matter of lizards and other dainty articles of food. He was about to lead his tribe in search of sustenance when they were attracted by loud screams. Instantly on guard, they stood watching the approach of the mad Thome. Nervous, irritable beasts, it was a question whether they would run away or attack, as the man dashed among them and threw himself on the ground, clutching the casket to his breast. For a moment they stood there, apparently undecided, their little, red rimmed eyes blazing; then they moved slowly away, their menacing growls lost upon the poor maniac.

"It is mine! It is mine!" he shrieked. "I am rich! In all the world there is none so rich as I!"

The great apes lumbered down the hillside, their short tempers upset by the screaming and jabbering of Thome, until Ungo was about to return and silence him forever. Just then he espied Brian and Lal Taask and transferred his anger from Thome to them. They were tarmangani, and suddenly Ungo wanted to kill all tarmangani.

Attracted by the growls of the anthropoids, the two men looked up and saw the herd charging down the hill toward them. "Those beasts mean business," cried Brian. "It's time we got out of here."

"There's a cave," said Lal Taask, pointing toward the cliff. "If we can reach it ahead of them, we may be able to hide from them. There's just a chance that they may be afraid to go into a dark hole like that."

Running at top speed, the men reached the cave long before the apes could overtake them. The interior was not entirely dark, and they could see that the cave extended beyond the range of their vision.

"We'd better go as far as we can," said Brian. "We'll be in a devil of a fix if they do come in and follow us; but perhaps if they can't see us at first, they may give up the chase."

"It may be a cul-de-sac," admitted Lal Taask, "but it was the only chance we had; they'd have had us sure if we'd stayed in the open."

They followed a dark corridor that ended suddenly in a magnificent grotto, the splendor of which fairly took their breath away.

"Great Scott!" exclaimed Brian. "Did you ever see anything so gorgeous?"

"It's magnificent," agreed Taask; "but, right now, quite incidental—the apes are coming! I hear them growling."

"There's another cave in the other side of this cavern," said Brian. "Let's try that."

"There is nothing else to try," returned Lal Taask.

As the two men disappeared into the dark opening in the rear of the cavern, Ungo and his fellows streamed into the chamber they had just quitted, unimpressed by its magnificence; and still holding to the idea that dominated them for the moment—the chase. A bug, a beetle, or a bat might distract their attention and launch them upon a new adventure, for they could not hold long to a single objective; but there were none of these, and so they searched the grotto for their quarry. They circled the place, looking behind stalagmites, sniffing here and there, wasting much time while the two men followed a new corridor deeper into the heart of the cliff.

31

TARZAN, D'ARNOT, HERKUF, and Lavac hastened through the air chamber out onto the bottom of the lake to the spot where Helen had been left to await their return; but she was not there, though the casket lay undisturbed where Herkuf had hidden it. There was no clew to her whereabouts; and the men were at a loss as to the direction in which they should search. They dared not separate, and so they followed Tarzan as he wandered here and there about the garden of the ptomes looking for some trace of the missing girl. While they were thus engaged, the ape-man's attention was attracted by the approach of several large marine animals the upper portions of which closely resembled the head and neck of a horse. There were six of them, and it was soon evident that they meant to attack. That they were extremely dangerous, Herkuf knew and the others soon realized, for they were as large as a man; and each was armed with a long, sharp horn which grew upward from the lower ends of their snouts.

Two of them attacked Tarzan, and one each the other three men, while the sixth circled about as though awaiting an opening through which it might take an antagonist unaware. Tarzan succeeded in dispatching one of those attacking him; and d'Arnot seemed to be experiencing no great difficulty with his. Lavac was hard pressed; but when he saw the sixth sea horse gliding up behind d'Arnot to impale him on its horn he turned to the rescue of his companion; as he did so, exposing himself to the attack of the sea horse with which he had been engaged.

It was an act of heroism on the part of the man who had wronged d'Arnot, an act that made full amends but cost a brave life, for the sea horse he had abandoned to come to d'Arnot's rescue plunged its powerful horn between his shoulders. Thus died Lieutenant Jacques La-vac.

As Tarzan thrust his trident into the heart of a second antagonist, the remaining beasts swam away in defeat. D'Arnot dropped to one knee beside Lavac and examined him as best he could; then he stood up and shook his head. The others understood; and sadly the three turned away and resumed their fruitless search, wondering, possibly, which would be the next to die in this land of danger and sudden death.

At last, by signs, they agreed to abandon the search, for even d'Arnot now felt certain that Helen must be dead; and, following Herkuf, who had brought the casket with him, they scaled the steep ascent to the lake shore, emerging at last a short distance below Ashair.

D'Arnot was heart broken; Herkuf was filled with renewed hope, for he knew what the casket contained and what it meant to him; only Tarzan of the Apes was unmoved. "Brulor is dead," he said, "and The Father of Diamonds stolen. I must return to Thobos as I promised Herat."

"It will not be necessary, if you wish to remain here and search for your other friends," said Herkuf. "I shall explain everything to Herat, and for what you have done to restore this to him, he will grant you any favor." He tapped the lid of the casket.

"What is it?" asked d'Arnot.

"In this is the true Father of Diamonds," replied Herkuf. "Many years ago, Chon, the true god, was making his annual tour of Holy Horus in a great galley. As was the custom, he carried The Father of Diamonds with him. Queen Atka, jealous of Herat, attacked and sank the galley; and Chon was drowned, while I was taken prisoner. As you, Tarzan, will recall, when we found the wrecked galley at the bottom of Horus, I recognized it and retrieved the casket that had lain there so many years. Now I am sure that if we restore The Father of Diamonds to Thobos, Herat will grant any request we may make, for without The Father of Diamonds, Thobos has been without a god all these years."

"You and Herkuf take the casket to Herat," said d'Arnot to Tarzan. "I cannot leave here. Helen may live and may come ashore. Somehow, I can't believe that she is dead."

"Take the casket to Herat, Herkuf," directed Tarzan. "I shall remain here with d'Arnot. Tell Herat I'll come back to Thobos if he wishes me to. I may come any way. We'll have to have a galley to get out of Tuen-Baka."

Herkuf made good time to Thobos, nor was there any delay on the part of Herat in granting him an audience when the king learned that he claimed to be the long lost priest, Herkuf, and that he had The Father of Diamonds in his possession; and it was not long after his arrival at the city gate before Herkuf stood before the king.

"Here, O Herat, is the sacred casket with The Father of Diamonds. Had it not been for the man, Tarzan, it would never have been recovered. I know that he and his friends are in grave peril, for they are close to Ashair. Will you not send galleys and warriors to rescue them?"

"With this," cried Herat, touching the casket, "our forces cannot lose, for we shall again have the god upon our side." He turned to one of his aides. "Let all the war galleys be prepared and manned. We shall attack Ashair at once; and at last the followers of the true god, Chon, shall prevail; and the traitors and the wicked shall be destroyed. All that is lacking to our complete triumph is the presence in the flesh of the holy Chon."

"He will be with us in spirit," Herkuf reminded him.

So King Herat put out from Thobos with many war galleys, to avenge the wrong that Atka had done his god and to succor the strangers who had been instrumental in recovering the true Father of Diamonds from the bottom of Holy Horus; and Queen Mentheb and her ladies waved to them from the quay and wished them godspeed.

*   *   *

The true god, Chon, and his priests were gathered in the cavern temple on the shore of Horus. The three prisoners stood below the altar before the throne. At a word from Chon, several priests seized Gregory, stripped his clothing from him, and threw him to his back across the altar. Chon rose from his throne and stood above him.

"From the entrails of this man let the oracle speak!"

181

he cried. He paused, and the priests intoned a weird chant, while Helen and Magra looked on, horrified and helpless.

"No! No!" cried Helen. "You must not! My father has done nothing to wrong you."

"Then why is he here in forbidden Tuen-Baka?" demanded Chon.

"I have told you time and again that we came here only in search of my brother, who is lost."

"Why was your brother here?"

"He came with a scientific expedition of exploration," explained the girl.

Chon shook his head. "It is death to all who enter forbidden Tuen-Baka from the outer world," he replied. "But we know why they really came. They came only for The Father of Diamonds. To us it is the emblem of godhood; to them it is a priceless object of incalculable value. There is nothing that they would not do to possess it. They would defile our temples; they would murder us. The fact that they could never succeed in obtaining it, does not lessen their guilt."

"My father would not have done these things. He only wanted his son back. He cares nothing for your diamond."

"There is no diamond where anyone can steal it," said Chon, "for The Father of Diamonds lies at the bottom of Horus, lost forever. If I am wrong in thinking that you came solely to steal it, you shall go free. I am a just god."

"But you *are* wrong," urged Helen. "Won't you please take my word for it? If you kill my father—oh, what good will it do you to find out later that you are wrong?"

"You may speak the truth," replied Chon, "but you may lie. The oracle will not lie. From the entrails of this man the oracle shall speak. Priests of the true god, prepare the sacrifice!"

As the priests stretched Gregory across the altar and sprinkled a liquid over him, the others commenced a solemn chant; and Helen stretched her arms toward Chon.

"Oh, please!" she begged. "If you must have a sacrifice, take me, not my father."

"Silence!" commanded Chon. "If you have lied, your time will come. Soon we shall know."

182

*　　*　　*

After Herkuf left them, Tarzan and d'Arnot started
back toward Ashair. They had no plan, nor much hope.
If Helen lived, she might be in Ashair. If she were dead,
d'Arnot did not care what fate befell him. As for Tarzan,
he was seldom concerned beyond the present moment. Suddenly he was alert. He pointed toward a cliff ahead of
them.

"One of Ungo's apes just went into that cave," he said.
"Let's take a look. The mangani are not ordinarily interested in caves. Something unusual may have impelled
that one to enter; we'll see what."

"Oh, why bother?" queried d'Arnot. "We are not interested in apes."

"I am interested in everything," replied the ape-man.

*　　*　　*

Brian and Taask stumbled through the dark corridor to
burst suddenly into the cavern temple upon the scene of
Gregory's impending sacrifice. At sight of them, Chon, the
true god, recoiled, dropping his knife hand at his side.

"In the name of Isis!" he shouted. "Who dares inter-
rupt?"

"Brian!" cried Helen.

"Helen!" The man started across the room toward his
sister; but half a dozen priests sprang forward and seized
him, and others intercepted Helen as she tried to run to
meet him.

"Who are these men?" demanded Chon.

"One is my brother," replied Helen. "Oh, Brian, tell
him we don't want their diamond."

"Save your breath, man," snapped Chon. "Only the
oracle speaks the truth! On with the sacrifice to truth!"

*　　*　　*

"Marvellous! Stupendous!" exclaimed d'Arnot, as he and
Tarzan entered the outer cavern of Chon's temple.

"Yes," admitted the ape-man, "but where is the man-
183

gani we saw coming in here. I smell many of them. They have just been in this cave. I wonder why?"

"Have you no soul?" demanded d'Arnot.

"I don't know about that," smiled Tarzan, "but I have a brain. Come on, let's get after those apes. I detect the scent spoor of men, too. The stink of the apes is so strong that it almost hides the other."

"I smell nothing," said d'Arnot, as he followed Tarzan toward the opening at the far end of the cavern.

* * *

Chon was furious. "Let there be no more interruptions!" he cried. "There are many questions to be asked of the oracle. Let there be silence, too; if the oracle is to be heard, the man must be opened in silence." Three times he raised and lowered the sacrificial knife above the prostrate Gregory. "Speak, oracle, that the truth may be known!"

As he placed the point of the knife at the lower extremity of the victim's abdomen, the great apes, led by Ungo, streamed into the cavern; and once again the rite of human sacrifice was interrupted, as Chon and his priests looked, probably for the first time, at these hairy beastmen.

The sight of so many tarmangani and the strange garments of the priests confused and irritated the apes, with the result that they attacked without provocation, forgetting the injunction of Tarzan.

The surprised priests, who had been holding Gregory, released him; and he slipped from the altar to stand leaning against it in a state bordering on collapse. Chon raised his voice in impotent curses and commands, while all the others tried to fight off the attacking apes.

Zu-tho and Ga-un saw the two girls, and Zu-tho recalled that Ungo had run off with a she tarmangani; so, impelled by imitative desire, he seized Magra; and Ga-un, following the lead of his fellow, gathered up Helen; then the two apes sought to escape from the cavern with their prizes. Being confused, they chanced upon a different corridor from that by which they had entered the cavern, a corridor that rose steeply to a higher level.

184

Before anyone had been seriously injured by the apes, a commanding voice rang out from the rear of the cavern. "Dan-do, mangani!" it ordered in a tongue no other human knew, and the great apes wheeled about to see Tarzan standing in the entrance to the cavern. Even Chon ceased his cursing.

Tarzan surveyed the gathering in the temple. "We are all here but Helen, Magra, and Lavac," he said, "and Lavac is dead."

"The girls were here a minute ago," said Gregory, as he hastily donned his clothes without interruption by Chon or the priests.

"They must have hidden somewhere when the apes came," suggested Brian.

"Helen was here!" gasped d'Arnot. "She is not dead?"

"She was here," Gregory assured him.

Brian was calling the girls loudly by name, but there was no reply. Chon was trying to gather his wits together.

* * *

Zu-tho and Ga-un dragged their captives through a steep, short corridor that ended in a third cavern with an arched opening that looked out over Horus far below. Zu-tho held Magra by the hair, while Ga-un dragged Helen along by one ankle. The apes stopped in the middle of the cavern and looked about. They didn't know what to do with their prizes now that they had them. They released their holds upon the girls and jabbered at one another, and as they jabbered, Helen and Magra backed slowly away from them toward the opening overlooking the lake.

"These are Tarzan's shes," said Zu-tho. "Ungo and Tarzan will kill us."

"Look at their hairless skins and little mouths," said Ga-un. "They are hideous and no good. If we kill them and throw them into the water, Tarzan and Ungo will never know that we took them."

Zu-tho thought that this was a good idea; so he advanced toward the girls, and Ga-un followed him.

"I kill!" growled Zu-tho, in the language of the great apes.

"I kill!" snarled Ga-un.

185

"I believe the beasts are going to kill us," said Magra.

"I can almost hope so," replied Helen.

"We'll choose our own death," cried Magra. "Follow me!"

As Magra spoke, she turned and ran toward the opening overlooking the lake; and Helen followed her. Zu-tho and Ga-un charged to seize them; but they were too late; and the girls leaped out into space over the waters of sacred Horus, far below; while Asharian warriors in a passing galley watched.

32

IN THE CAVERN temple, Chon had finally regained control of his shattered nerves. He could curse again, and he did. "Curses on all who defile the temple of Chon, the true god," he cried.

"Chon!" exclaimed Tarzan. "But Chon is dead."

"Chon is not dead," replied the god. "I am Chon!"

"Chon was drowned when his galley was sunk, many years ago," insisted the ape-man.

"What do you know of all this?" demanded Chon.

"I know what Herkuf told me," replied Tarzan, "and he was a priest of Chon."

"Herkuf!" exclaimed Chon. "Does he live?"

"Yes, Chon; he is on his way now to Thobos with the casket of The Father of Diamonds which we found in the wreck of your galley at the bottom of Horus."

"Thanks be to Isis!" exclaimed Chon. "When Atka's galleys attacked us," he went on to explain, "I donned my water suit and helmet and leaped overboard. Thus I escaped, and eventually I found this cavern. Here I have lived for many years, watching my chance to capture ptomes from the temple of the false Brulor—ptomes who were still at heart faithful to the true god. If you have spoken the truth you shall all go free with my blessing."

"First of all," said Tarzan, "we must find the girls. D'Arnot, you come with me. Ungo, bring the mangani. The rest of you search the main corridor," and so the survivors set out in search of the missing girls, while Chon and his priests chanted a prayer for the safe return of The Father of Diamonds.

* * *

As the Asharians saw the girls leap into the water, the officer in charge of the galley directed that its course be changed; and it was rowed rapidly in their direction. Helen and Magra saw it coming and tried to find a place where they could gain the shore and escape, for they knew that there would be only enemies in the galley; but the precipitous cliff that fronted the lake at this point made escape impossible. The galley overtook them, and they were soon dragged into the craft.

"By Brulor!" exclaimed one of the Asharians. "This is the woman who murdered Zytheb, keeper of the keys of the temple. Atka will reward us well for this, for it was, doubtless, this woman who also contrived the flooding of the temple and the drowning of all within it."

Magra looked at Helen. "What more can happen to us?" she asked wearily.

"This must be the absolute end," replied Helen, "and I hope it is. I am very tired."

When they finally reached the city and were taken into Atka's presence, the Queen scowled horribly at them and pointed at Helen. "It was because of you," she cried, "that the temple was flooded and all the priests and handmaidens drowned. I cannot think of any punishment adequate to your crime, but I shall. Take them away!"

In the dungeon in which they were chained, they sat looking at one another, rather hopelessly. "I wonder how long it will take her to think up a punishment to fit the crime," said Helen. "Too bad she can't call in Gilbert and Sullivan."

Magra smiled. "I am glad you can joke," she said. "It makes it much easier to endure."

187

"Why not joke while we can?" asked Helen. "We shall soon be dead, and death is no joke."

* * *

The mad Thome wandered aimlessly near the banks of Horus, jabbering constantly of the things his great wealth would purchase from the fleshpots of Europe. He had no idea where Europe was nor how to reach it. He only recalled that it was a place where one might satisfy the cravings of every appetite. He was so engrossed in his mad dreaming that he did not see Taask approaching.

The Indian had been searching for Helen; and had become separated from Gregory and Brian, when suddenly he came upon Atan Thome and saw the casket in his hands. Instantly he sloughed every thought but one—to get possession of the accursed thing that held the priceless diamond. Sneaking up on Thome, he leaped upon him. They rolled upon the ground, biting, kicking, and clawing. Taask was a younger, stronger man; and he soon wrenched the casket from Atan Thome; and, leaping to his feet, started to run away with it.

Screaming at the top of his voice, the madman picked up a rock and pursued him. There was murder in the eyes and heart of Atan Thome as he chased his erstwhile servant across the rocky ground above Ashair. Seeing that he could not overtake Lal Taask, Atan Thome hurled the rock at him; and by chance it struck the fleeing man full on the head, knocking him to the ground; and his mad pursuer was soon upon him. Recovering the rock, Thome pounded with all his strength upon the skull of Lal Taask until it was but a mass of splintered bone and brains; then, clutching the casket to his breast and screaming a challenge to the world, he fled.

* * *

Following the scent spoor of the two girls, Tarzan and d'Arnot found themselves in a third cavern of the temple, facing two bull apes.

"Where are the shes?" demanded Tarzan.

Zu-tho pointed toward the lake. "They jump," he said, "in water."

Tarzan looked out to see the Asharian galley rowing in the direction of the city; then he and d'Arnot returned to the throne room and related what they had seen. "I am going to take the apes to Ashair," he said. "With their help, I may be able to bring the girls out."

"My priests shall go with you," said Chon, and the party soon set out from the temple, the men armed with tridents and knives, the apes with their terrible fangs and their mighty muscles.

* * *

An excited warrior rushed into the throne room of Atka and knelt before her. "O Queen!" he cried, "a great fleet of war galleys is approaching from Thobos."

Atka turned to one of her aides. "Order out the entire fleet," she directed. "This day we shall destroy the power of Thobos forever."

As the Asharian horde embarked at the quay, Tarzan of the Apes looked down from the hillside above the city and watched them; and in the distance, approaching Ashair, he saw the war fleet of Herat approaching.

"Now is the time," he said to his motley followers, "we shall have fewer warriors to oppose us."

"We cannot fail," said a priest, "for Chon has blessed us."

A few minutes later the Lord of the Jungle led his little band over the wall into The Forbidden City. It was a bold, rash venture—at best a forlorn hope that thus they might succeed in saving Helen and Magra from death or an even more horrible fate. Success or failure—which would it be?

* * *

As the two fleets met amid the war cries of the opposing warriors, quarter was neither asked nor given, for each side felt that this was to be a battle to the death that would determine for all time which city was to rule the valley of Tuen-Baka. And while this bloody battle was being waged on sacred Horus, another battle was taking place before the gates of Atka's palace, as Tarzan sought to lead his little band into the presence of the Queen. It was Atka he sought, for he knew that with Atka in his power he could force the Asharians to give up their prisoners—if they still lived.

Finally they overcame the resistance at the gates, and Tarzan forced his way at the head of his company into the throne room of the Queen.

"I have come for the two women," he said. "Release them to me, and we will go away; refuse, and we shall go away; but we shall take you with us."

Atka sat in silence for a few minutes, her eyes fixed upon Tarzan. She was trembling slightly and appeared to be making an effort to gain control over her emotions. At last she spoke. "You have won," she said. "The women shall be fetched at once."

As Tarzan and his triumphant band led the girls from Ashair, Magra clung to his arm. "Oh, Tarzan," she whispered, "I knew that you would come. My love told me that you would."

The ape-man shook his head impatiently. "I do not like such talk," he said; "it is not for us. Leave that to Helen and Paul."

* * *

Herat, victorious, entered Ashair, the first king of Thobos to set foot within The Forbidden City. From the opening in the cavern of Chon, that looked out over the lake, Chon had seen the Asharian fleet demolished and the victorious Thobotian fleet steer toward Ashair; and when Tarzan and his party returned and the ape-man learned of the successful outcome of Herat's expedition, he had Chon send a messenger to Ashair to summon Herat, in the true god's name, to the temple.

When the greetings between Herat and Chon were concluded, the true god blessed the entire party, giving credit to the strangers for their part in the restoration of The Father of Diamonds to the temple of Chon and the successful reuniting of the King and the true god; then Herat, to demonstrate his own appreciation, offered to outfit the Gregory party and furnish them with galleys to take them out of Tuen-Baka. At last, their troubles seemed over.

"We are reunited and safe," said Gregory, "and, above all others, we owe it to you, Tarzan. How can we ever repay you?"

Gregory was interrupted by maniacal screams, as two of Herat's warriors who had been among the guard left at the outer entrance to the caverns, entered the temple, dragging Atan Thome between them.

"This man has a casket," reported one of the warriors, "which he says contains The Father of Diamonds."

"The true Father of Diamonds, which Herkuf just brought with him from Thobos," said Chon, "rests here in its casket on the altar before me. There cannot be two. Let us have a look at what the man has in his casket."

"No!" shrieked Atan Thome. "Don't open it! It is mine, and I have been waiting to open it in Paris. I shall buy all of Paris with it and be king of France!"

"Silence, mortal!" commanded Chon; then, very deliberately, he opened the casket, while the trembling Thome stared with mad eyes at the contents—a small lump of coal.

At sight of it, realizing what it was, Atan Thome screamed, clutched his heart, and fell dead at the foot of the altar of the true god.

"For this false and accursed thing," exclaimed Brian Gregory, "we have all suffered, and many have died; yet the irony of it is that it is, in truth, The Father of Diamonds."

"Men are strange beasts," said Tarzan.

ABOUT EDGAR RICE BURROUGHS

Edgar Rice Burroughs is one of the world's most popular authors. With no previous experience as an author, he wrote and sold his first novel—*A Princess of Mars*—in 1912. In the ensuing thirty-eight years until his death in 1950, Burroughs wrote 91 books and a host of short stories and articles. Although best known as the creator of the classic *Tarzan of the Apes* and *John Carter of Mars*, his restless imagination knew few bounds. Burroughs' prolific pen ranged from the American West to primitive Africa and on to romantic adventure on the moon, the planets, and even beyond the farthest star.

No one knows how many copies of ERB books have been published throughout the world. It is conservative to say, however, that of the translations into 32 known languages, including Braille, the number must run into the hundreds of millions. When one considers the additional world-wide following of the Tarzan newspaper feature, radio programs, comic magazines, motion pictures and television, Burroughs must have been known and loved by literally a thousand million or more.